The Daily Journal of Arabella Crumblestone

A Children's Story

by

Sharon King

with love
Sharon King
x

MIDNIGHT

OWL BOOKS

First published 2010 by Midnight Owl Books
ISBN: 978-0-9567413-0-1

Illustrations by Rose King

Typeset, Printed and Bound by
www.beamreachuk.co.uk

for Rose, Daisy & Lenny,

with all my love

Paint My Heart a Different Colour

Paint my heart a different colour
It is grey
Fill it with fondness for a friend
Let that friend stay
Let her hold my cold and crumbling hand
And share the wonders of this land
So that the world is filled with sunlight
Every day

The Daily Journal of Arabella Crumblestone

27th October
The sun a bright burning coin in the near, Autumnal Sky

Today, I started my new life. I came out through a gap in the stone wall and hitched a ride on the undercoat of a huge sheep named Leroy. I will not tell you what came before, because I cannot. I do not know if you believe that, or if you fancy me a truth-twister. And who are you anyhow? An invisible somebody on the other side of the scraps of paper that I find here and there. I write upon them with a dark, burned twig. I write and I write and I hold onto these writings for fear of forgetting again. If I knew you, if I trusted you, I could tell you parts of my story. If I had a friend. This is the point of it all, you see. I have no friend here in the wall, and my stone heart calls out for company.

So, here you find me, clinging to the white, matted undercoat, breathing in the warm, damp sheep-smell. Perhaps it is a smell that you would dislike. To me, escaping from a dusty, cold eternity, Leroy's is the smell of Life.

Breathing deep of the 'tumnal air, I promised my great woollen steed that we would remain friends no matter what, and that he would be rewarded for his kindness. Of the promise that I spoke, I would guess he had no notion. Nothing seems to register in the sideways on oblong eyes, but Leroy's heart, I sense, is good.

28th October

A great mist has fallen from the heavens. It is not shocking to me, little thing that I am, made purely of the elements. My delicate body is used to the cold and the harshness. Still, I crawl deeper into Leroy's matted coat, loving the animal warmth that he gives. There is no food for me here. Lichen and moss are what I crave. You may think that sounds like a limited diet, and you may be right. Let me tell you a little about moss though. If you are thinking of it as a single, green, carpet without variety then you are badly wrong! Take up my challenge. Look closely at the mosses and lichens which grow in abundance on stony walls. Miniature forests, I lie to you not! Rich greens, reds, browns. Tiny, swaying trees spilling forth clouds of nutrition at a touch. There are the long brown fronds, which taste tangy and sour. Seeds like groundnuts. Oh, there is much to be said for the fruits of the wall, only they are not here, and my stone belly is empty.

I will learn to try new foods. I know it now, I will need to!

29th October
No reprieve from the perpetual fog

Leroy will go no further! He is owned, not his own beast at all. He sees an invisible boundary in this land, where I see none. I shall go on alone.

2

30th October

So, dear invisible reader, my only friend, Leroy, is gone. He didn't leave me; I did him! How lonely a life without his dirty, warm animal smell. My steps are tiny compared with his determined and four-footed ones, and I dare not stop for too long to forage for food. The hunger in my belly rages on. Night draws in so soon after the day has dawned and sometimes I find myself feeling fond regret of my gap in the wall. But there are many gaps, and the wall goes on forever.

31st October
Faerie

How can I tell you what I am? The nearest thing I can compare myself to in the knowledge of your world is faerie. I am made of stone, however. Statue? No! I am no statue. My body is of the stone, but I have delicate, folded wings of stuff more comparable to human skin, or of the feather of birds; maybe somewhere velvet-in-between. I know not how to use these soft and folded wings. Tonight as I look to the dark blue sky with the half- moon hanging sadly, I know that soon I must find out. The wings do not feel part of me! I so miss Leroy and his warm fleece.

1st November
A boy who hums

The air has turned with the new month, and I have made human contact. A boy! A straight-hearted boy who knows no words but offered me sustenance in the form of a sweet, brown cube. Seasoned with my hunger, this cube tasted better than anything I have eaten in my whole life. I took it in my two stone hands and chomped! The sweet and creamy gloop of it! My goodness! I could not will my eyes open, as I sailed on the dream of its taste! Eventually, I asked the boy his name. He smiled widely and issued a curious humming noise, which I feel certain cannot be his name. I heard and felt the hum, it rumbled right through me and shivered my useless wings. An adult came by and kindly led the boy off by the hood, so I hid, sated and dreamy in the shadows of the wall.

2nd November
The girl

Today the boy's sister came to the wall with him. Her hair is brown and shiny as a conker; shinier still. She is different than him, I feel. She speaks constantly, chattering, chattering.

"What have you seen, George? Is it a rabbit? D'you want to show Faith? Ooh, look, long grass. You like long grass, don't you Georgy?"

Still, I hide. Today the air is even colder, and promises a real freeze. With my dusty heart, I can endure much, I know it. But the loneliness! I need a friend. Can I trust these humanchildren.

3rd November
Decisions

The children are gone and here is I, left to the heartlessness of hedgehogs and spiders. Onwards I go for there is no turning back for me now. Decisions is decisions and, with the sweet taste of the boy's offerings still on my tongue, I make by bed on the light-dewy moss of this stone wall. I have a little taste of it but the moss is chewy and nothing to me now. Spoiled is me, from the taste of George's gift!

My only plan – "Follow the wall, Arabella Crumblestone." It must lead to summat!

4th November
A colourful burst of fire in the sky; could it be a sign?

'Scuse me, for I can only write at night, daytimes being for surviving. Darkness is here once again, and the humanchildren are back. I heard and felt the vibration of a rumbling grumbling racket as their vehicle approached. Another sweet creamy square from George melted me into a pool of gratification! I made myself known to the girl child. I have nothing to lose! (oh, how you tell lies to your own self, Arabella, you know nothing of the world, what there is or what there is not to lose). I came forth from the wall and looked directly at Faith, trying to stand tall and proud on the loose stones of the ancient wall.

I don't think I fooled her. I felt so shamed, the dusty, crumbling, useless-wingness of me. But she smiled so wide and true and I could barely help but to hop onto her outstretched hand. Many questions she could have asked of my nature, who was I? What was I? Did I have a family? I feigned dumbness for want of what to tell. She searched my soul with her sparkling green eyes and then stuffed me in her pocket.

Her smell was different to Leroy's, but good nonetheless. A friend! I have a friend on this cold, dark night. I have a bed in her warm pocket. What more could I ask for?

5th November
Unbelievable, amidst the fires and the booms, I know that my life has truly begun

I remained, safe and warm in the comfortable net of Faith's pocket. We were inside the vessel that she calls

'Car' for such a very long, sleepy time. It rumbled on and on and shook the very stone essence of me. Faith peered down at me every now and then, sometimes prodding. She chats away. I do not answer, though.

She tells me that sometimes, she too is afraid, and that for as long as I like I can hide deep away from the world, with my hands over my pointed ears. I pretend to not know the meaning of her whispered words, and I stare back at her, wide-eyed and fearful.

But when we left the Car, and were out in the blue night air, she showed me the colours in the sky! Never before have I seen such a sight. The pale moon cries, ashamed of her bleak-yellow drabness while I, Arabella Crumblestone, perch, half terrified and half gleeful and look with wonder at the strange world that is now mine!

6th November
Encaged!

Here I am now in the cage of a rat rodent named 'Albert Einstein'.

"Stay here", Faith said to me, so sincere and secretive.

I! I who can move through the very stuff of stone! She fancies those bars will hold me. Alby, the rat, is not unkind, with his elderberry eyes, but the cooling pools of bright yellow urine around his cage are unacceptable to me. The cage is in a low-ceilinged room which contains a fancy bed, an effigy of a large horse, and many, many books. I long to explore the room, but Faith has instructed me to stay in here with the rat. I smile nervously at him and he twitches his whiskers. Oh, Faith, my conker haired friend, I shall have to shed my cloak of dumbness and have serious talks with you!

7th November
A Serious Talk and a Wondrous Gift

I looked at my new friend and she looked at me. She chatters so mostly, but with her hand full of rich nutritional cubes and crumbs for Alby and me, and a small smile on her rose hued lips, she seemed to sense that I would speak first.

"Your hair is wondrous", I dared to say. My own hair is nothing to speak of. I have a few long and straggly strands, the colour of pondweed. Mostly bald is my dusty head, with large, dark eyes dominating my face.

"So. You *can* talk," she says to me, with a smile that tells me she knew so all along.

"Aye, Faith," says I, coming to the bars of the cage all wide eyed and terrified. "And let me tell you, I cannot stand to be caged here with your foul-smelling pet."

Faith undid the hatch and took me out of the cage in an instant. She held me close to her warmth and I must confess a tear made tracks in the dust of my petrous face. I had remained silent, in fear of her questions, imagining that they would fire at me like hard hail on a windy day; but the questions never came. Just the warmth of her and my wet tears between us.

I showed her the rolled up pages of my diary, and after reading them carefully, she commented upon the beauty of my name and marched away, so determined. She came back soon with a gift for me. Such a gift! It is customary for humans to swap gifts. I had given her the truth of my spoken word, and she gave me a real book in return! Bejewelled, an' all. Tiny it was to her (she told me that the Tooth Faerie had exchanged it for her first baby tooth), but just the right size for me. A tiny pencil nestles snugly in its spine. The pencil is thick for my small, stone hand, but manoeuvrable, and far easier to read than the burned stick etchings. So now I write like a lady; though lady I am not. I am nought. That is how I feel. But at least I have a friend to share my nothingness with.

"Live in my dolls' house, Arabella. It's gorgeous!"

I nodded and nodded and smiled as prettily as a stone person such as myself can. She carried me to Dolls' House and opened the door. I found the place crammed with strange effigies of animals, which were adorned with clothing and other human paraphernalia.

"There's no room for me, Faith," I said to her, and she immediately cleared the effigies away, leaving perhaps one or two of them which she said where her favourites.

"To keep you company."

So now I have a place to live. A warm place that is neither a gap in a wall or a cage full of claws and urine. I have a friend, and soon I will have clothes, for Faith has said she will make me some.

A momentous day!

8th November

Together, Faith and I have re-arranged the furniture in Dolls' House. She works so much faster than I, scooping huge handfuls of the strange belongings away, saying that I may not find them useful. In truth none of these things are useful to me; so light and flimsy! I do not tell her this. She empties handfuls of it into bags that are flimsier still, and shoves them into the cupboards in the walls that surround this room.

Now she is gone. I choose to sit upon the wooden floor of Dolls' House, rather than on the light chair that she guided me to.

Faith tells me the names of the rich foodstuffs that she brings to me. Cheeses. Crackers. McDonalds. This food makes me feel sleepy, and sometimes a fragrant patch of moss is all that I crave.

I say nothing of these cravings, nor of my constant drowsiness and inability to sleep properly. I just smile, smile, and smile.

My new clothes are simple and sewn with Faith's giant stitches, a ribbon around my tiny waist, matching the one that draws back my tired scrapings of hair.

There is a mirror in Dolls' House. I see myself often, and in truth I am not so cheered by the reflection.

Miserable creatures both are my reflection and I! Warm though, and I do like Faith so. Maybe we need more talks.

9th November
A Frightening Day

Most of the day Faith is gone and at evening times she returns with foodstuffs and conversation for me. Plenty of reflection time for Arabella Crumblestone in between! I sit with my thoughts and the animal effigies stare back at me, emptiness in their unmoveable eyes. A scratching and a squeaking of the wheel sometimes reminds me of

Alby's presence. I hear the rain sounds from the outer world, a world that was once my own. I have my beautiful diary, crusted with pink and white jewels. I have all the time in the world to write down my ramblings. The days are stretched out far and I long to hear the eager clatter of Faith's steps on the wooden boards.

The footfalls were heavier today, but I did not bother to ask myself the question 'to whom do they belong?' The steps were slower than Faith's, I realise this now that I am thinking clearly. Into the room pounded a big human dressed in greys and blues – I saw her through the square window of Dolls' House. I hid with my back to the wooden wall, in the corner's shadow, the little drum of my heart picking up speed.

"Faith Raymondson!" I heard her say crossly. I wondered briefly if she was insane, for Faith was not there at all!

From the negligible safety of the shadows, I saw her hand, large with green shiny fingernails. A monster hand! It scooped up scattered pieces and animal statues from Dolls' House. Thundering steps, made louder by her anger! She came closer. I could feel the floorboards shake beneath her stomping feet. My stone heart stood still as the large front door of Dolls' House was yanked open.

Was I found? Would I be captured? Tortured? Ground down to dust? None of these! She did not even look inside, but crammed the pieces of furniture into Dolls' House, before quickly shutting the door again. For a while she remained in the room, moving things, sighing deeply; sweeping the wooden floor. I came closer to the window and I watched as she dismantled Alby's cage, cleaning its bottom tray with many white handkerchiefs that she then dropped into a large black bag. She sprayed a substance that, even from my hiding place, made my eyes water, and the pricklings of a sneeze threatened to betray me.

When at last her heavy footfalls retreated, I lay down on a hard, wooden bed. This bed is covered with a single checked green blanket, so light it offers me no comfort or warmth. I waited for Faith to return.

10th November

Today was much the same as yesterday, only no visit from the angry giantess. Faith tells me that this giant lady is her mother, and that she likes things spotless. I explored each room of Dolls House, climbing nimbly through the gaps in the wood that represent windows. I tried to sleep. My body is weary from all the travelling and my mind is fizzing with the details of my new experiences. Each time I close my eyes I see an image of the Giantess.

She is Faith's mother. And my Mother? I know not where she is.

11th November

Today was the same again. I have food and warmth, but am still so tired. Faith has brought me a soft bag that smells of outside and freshness. It is far more comfortable than the wooden bed. Lavender Bag, she calls it. With my head resting lightly on this soft and fragrant bed, I am determined that I will, at last, fall to sleep.

12th November

No sleep again last night. Faith feels that I have grown ill in the days that she has known me. During her visit to me today, a tear formed in the rim of her green eye, spilling over the edge and splattering on the wooden floor near my bed. I dint cry but watched the patterns that her tear made, soaking into the delicate grain of the wood. I looked up at her from my soft, Lavender bed.

"I'll have a little sleep," I told her. "That will make me better".

She came back later with a dish of red liquid warmth that she called Soup. It was thick and the sweet smell of it filled the whole of the room. Faith ate a little to encourage me. She found an Arabella sized spoon in the kitchen of Dolls House, but the spoon end was completely flat and the warm liquid slipped straight off. To cheer my friend, I dragged myself up and perched on one side of the blue pottery dish. My little licks of the soup tasted of real goodness. I slurped and even gulped a few mouthfuls. When I looked up and smiled at Faith she giggled, and plucked the mirror from the wooden wall to show me my reflection. I laughed a little too, seeing the red splodges adorning my grey face.

Looking closer though, I hardly recognised the Arabella in the smoky mirror! Her features were flatter than mine, and less well defined. Her nose was hardly there at all, and her eyes too far back in her stone head.

I gasped.

"Faith. I am crumbling away!"

13th November

So tired today, this pen feels heavy. I will try to sleep now.

14th November
Sickness

Again, forgive me. So very tired. The page and the world swim before my eyes and bright flickering lights obscure my vision.

15th November

I spent many hours drifting in and out of confusion. Blue eyes like two kind pools looked down upon me. I longed to dive into them. I smiled weakly and heard a commotion.

"George, NO! Come away from there right now!"

It was George, the boy, the Giver of Chocolate! He turned away and I could no longer see his kind blue eyes. Faith was so cross with him, she pulled him roughly away from Dolls' House and spoke words like harsh, stinging raindrops.

"I said away! You must not come into my bedroom George!"

George, strong boy that he is, pushed back at Faith, and she fell to the wooden floor, landing neatly on her bottom.

"Ow!" protested my friend.

I struggled to keep my eyes open, even amid such drama as this. Humming loudly all the while, George touched my crumbling face tenderly with the tips of his sturdy fingers. His touch was cool and soothing, and looking into the clear blue of his eyes was like falling into the sky. From his pocket he took a clump of rich green moss, a densely packed morsel with tall brown fronds. He lay it on the soft bag that is my bed, and the fresh, clean smell of it seemed to sharpen my mind. I remained there for a moment or two breathing in the outdoor smell of it, and then propped myself up on one arm.

Now two pairs of huge, kind eyes looked down upon me. The first blue as a summer sky and the other a dark and sparkling green.

"Oh, George, you clever boy" whispered Faith. "Arabella needs to be outside!"

16th November
Search for a suitable wall

Faith took me today outside to the wider world. Immediately, I started to recover. Only when the fog in my mind began to clear did I have an idea of how extremely ill I had become. Now I wear a cape that Faith has sewn for me. It is made of light brown fur, with strings to tie at the neck. I like the feel of it; very grand it is. Breathing in the crisp freshness of the outdoor air, not contaminated by the stinging cleaning spray, or the overpowering smell of rat urine, I feel like me again. I feel alive and excited.

I asked Faith to take me to the wall, her steps being much bigger than mine. She was puzzled at first, until I reminded her that the wall was where she had first found me.

"But that wall's not here, Arabella" she told me. "We were away on holiday when George found you there."

The wall not here? It is hard for me to accept that the wall is not everywhere, like the sky and the grass. My wall, all I have known, is far away, and Faith cannot take me there. She would need a Car Journey, she explains, and such a journey can be organised by adults only.

"Another wall, then?" I asked her, bleakly.

"Yes. Of course. Another wall."

The wall that she took me to first of all was so strange. It was hardly a wall at all. There were no gaps! Or true to say there *were* gaps, but these were filled with softer, more crumblesome stone. Many regular edged stones nestled close together, leaving no room for me to hide. There was no moss or lichen at all. I shook my head sadly, and Faith tried again.

She could not venture too far afield, she told me, as this would make her mother angry. Eventually, I sighed heavily, accepting a wall of uneven stones and textures, but sadly lacking in gaps. I walked straight into the wall, merging the stone that I am with its rubble. I can do this, you know. It takes effort, and I move through some textures more easily than others, but it is worth it! The minerals of the stones flowed straight into me - they gave me strength and mended my wrongs in an instant.

From the dark heart of the stone, I could hear my friend

calling my name, fancying me gone forever.

I poked my head out from the earthy depths and smiled widely at her. "Leave me here for tonight, Faith," I told her. "Come back for me tomorrow and I will be well again. And thank you!"

21st November

Dearest Arabella,

I know that you are still inside the wall, because I see the spine edge of your diary and a corner from your fur cape embedded within the mortar. Please forgive me, my lovely little friend. I never knew how ill being inside the house would make you. I did not mean to imprison you in my dolls' house, I just thought it would be a safe place for you to live.

I know that you are not an animal (though really I am not sure what you are, Arabella), but I have been thinking how wrong it is for wild animals to be caged in zoos and circuses, and I know in my heart that it was wrong for you to be caged in my dolls' house (and in Alby's cage – will you ever forgive me for that?). You said you would come back out of the wall the very next day, and now five days have gone without me seeing your darling face. Will I ever see you again?

Can we remain friends? This is my dearest wish.

My heart is missing you so terribly.

Your loving friend,

Faith Verity Raymondson
xxxx

22nd November
A new beginning

Today I emerged, brand new, from the wall. There was a humanchild waiting for me as I came from the stone. I scarcely had time to shake the dust from my stone body, let alone to hide from her, so I spoke instead, feeling strong and brave, not knowing or caring if she were friend or foe!

"Pleased to meet you," says I, "I am Faith Rumblestone!"

"Arabella?" The humanchild seemed confused.

"Who is this Arabella that you speak of? My name is Faith. I remember it clearly. What is *your* name, brown haired humanchild?"

She assured me that my name was, indeed, Arabella, and reasoned that my memory must be failing me. Together we read through the pages of a jewelled journal, which she kindly dug out of the wall with a rusty green garden trowel. Amid a cascade of mortar dust, I read the truth of my life!

Arabella. This, of course, is my name! Faith is my friend! The sparkle in her green eyes tugs the fragile strings of my memory. She is sure that I need to go into the stone to sleep and to stay healthy, but fears that each time I do, my memories may fail me. What am I to do? I want to stay well, but at the same time, to keep my own self, name and all! I shall write again tomorrow, though what I might fancy my name to be then, only the moon knows for sure!

23rd November

Hello, dear invisible reader, this is me, Edna Gardengnome! Ha ha! It is a joke! Good fortune is mine for I know who I am! Today was bright but Wintersome. I spent only an hour inside the stone of the wall last night, leaving a corner from my brown fur cape lolling like a rude tongue from the stones. This, my clever and kind friend Faith tugged upon, first gently and then a little more insistently, until I emerged, good as new but all recollections safely intact.

I feel healthy and powerful, Queen of the Stones!

Faith is so happy that I am well and that I will not have to leave her, and I, in return, am grateful that each emergence from the wall does not bring me forth confused and empty. What adventures Faith and I will have now that we have solved this problem!

24th November

The nights are long. They are cold and exciting. A real fox flashed its silver, twin-moon eyes at me last night. For a moment, my eyes and his were locked. He broke away first, turning quickly and disappearing into the undergrowth. There were other scurryings too. The night is alive with visitors! When I become too tired I rest within a nest of leaves that Faith has swept against the corner meeting of two walls. It is crunchy and nice in there, with delicious smells of autumn gone, and the mould that clings to older things.

I can't help wishing that Faith were just the size of me and that she could sleep out here under the quarter moon, breathing in the clear, velvet air of the night. But no, of course, it is not to be. Nothing could allow for that, her mother especially! So cross she seems, much of the time. Faith tells me that her mother's mind is full of worries for George, who hums instead of speaking and refuses to learn about the human world. Faith is sad when she tells me of George's troubles, and I carefully hold back my questions.

We are planning an adventure, Faith and I. The jacket that she wears for schooling each day (which she calls Blazer) has a hidden pocket on the inside, silky and cool to touch. She tells me how easily I could fit in there and be her secret for a day.

"Not every day though, Faith" I said to her, not wanting to offend, but thinking of my illness in the Dolls' House days.

"No! One day only, and we have breaks outdoors. You would only be inside for an hour or two the whole day! It'll be brilliant fun!"

Brilliant to me is a perfectly round sun making itself known through the thin but freezing cloud of a Winter's morning. Not a pocket or a schooling room. I must learn to expect the best and the best may greet me more often. Our adventure is tomorrow. I will write if I am not too tired by it.

25th November
School day adventure

For the first day in my confused and broken little life, I have been to school. Surely if I had ever been to such a place before the memory would have stuck, firm and safe in my dusty little mind!

So many people I never could have imagined. So much

chatter amid the thunder of a thousand feet. No one would have seen me at all so busy were they, but there was Arabella Crumblestone, her grey head peeking from the breast pocket of Faith's blazer. Faith wanted to introduce me to Greta, a tall and blue-eyed friend of hers who is now a friend of us both. She can be trusted with the secret of me, of this Faith is sure.

"What is it?" Greta asked, when Faith first pulled me out of her pocket in the quiet cloak area.

"She's not an *it*!" Faith whispered, harshly, "are you, Arabella?"

I did not have the courage to speak, but shook my head, slowly.

"How are you doing that?" Greta asked, suspiciously.

"Greta, meet Arabella Crumblestone! She's real, you nit! She's a faerie. Hang on a minute, are you a faerie, Arabella?"

I dint know the answer to this question but nodded quickly.

The two girls sat down on a bench, backed by a waterfall of different coloured coats and bags. "Let's have a look", Greta said, holding out her hand and looking a little concerned.

"Well, ok, but she's not a toy".

"I'm definite not a toy!" says I brightly, hopping on to the bigger girl's outstretched hand before she had the chance to grab me. Foolish me, for the shock of my tiny voice made her pull back her hand. I fell to the floor of School and shut my eyes in fear of the painful crash that would be my landing. The crash never came and my fall slowed down as though I were in a dream. Faith must have been lightning quick, or I must have been feather-fall slow. I don't know which, but she managed to catch me before I broke to a thousand stony crumbs on that hard and shiny floor.

"I'm really sorry!" Greta said, looking closely at me. "Are you ok? I've never met a faerie before."

26th November
Outdoors and Indoors

Ungrateful little me. Faith asked me to go to School again with her today, but I said no. Perhaps stone hearts are not made for friendship. The indoor places where Faith spends her time make me so tired. The bright light that comes from neither sun, moon nor stars. The toasty warmth in the heart of winter. It seems all wrong to me, but what do I know? Hardly anything at all, and that is the shocking truth. It is nighttime now. I sit here writing amid my nest of leaves which have been sodden and dry so many times that they have almost lost their leaf shapes.

Faith has already visited, just before dark. She brought me a real mushroom, which I devoured and it didn't make me ill, not even a little. I am full and well and the bright stars are winking their secret messages, but I find it hard to be restful. Have I upset Faith with my refusals? Friendship can be a troublesome business. I can only wait until I see her tomorrow.

27th November
Indoors again

Faith's mother does not like for her to spend too much time out in the garden, with the Winter being here.

"What are you doing out there?" she shouts every so often from the open door leading to Dining Room. The harsh light from indoors spills out into the garden, but does not reach the wall and my pile of leaves.

"I should go in soon," Faith said sadly tonight.

"Perhaps I could come to your room for a short time?" I suggested.

"I'll open the window to stop you from feeling ill!" Faith grinned wide and kissed my cheek.

She took me up to her familiar attic room. She flicked at the wall and all was dark. It took our night eyes some moments to gain strength, but when they did, Faith pulled at a cord and opened the window up above. The starlight and fragrant air flooded the room, and even Alby, the rat, stopped running around his wheel endlessly. He sat upright and sniffed, his whiskers twitching at the beauty of the night.

28th November

So here I am again outdoors. I am out and I am in, out and in! Can you ever keep track of me! Greta came to play tonight. She is full of sorrows and apologies for dropping me to the School floor. She brought me a gift to say as much, a tiny crown made from rose thorns. They are stuck into a moulded green ring which fits my head perfectly.

Faith brought out the little mirror from Dolls' House to show me how I looked. I gasped, hardly recognising the smoky but beautiful Queen Arabella. My features are sharp and defined again. Where thin snakes of hair once hung sadly, now a rich green cascade tumbles gloriously around my shoulders. I shook my head, and the crown remained steady. I felt a little stirring and dancing within myself.

29th November

To wile away the long days while Faith, Greta and George are at school I play a little flying game. I climb the craggy rocks of my wall, and jump. Each time I dare myself to climb a little higher. I mark the height from where I have jumped with a twig, which I stick into the stone of the wall.

The most daring height from which I have descended is marked at a third of the way up this wall. Looking up now from the ground I can only just see the marker!

I didn't fly though. Maybe these shabby and crinkly wings are for decoration only. Maybe I should ask Faith to snip them off with her sewing scissors and make me a pair of prettier ones.

Time and again I climb the wall and brave the jump, spreading out my cape of fur to act as a parachute. It is fun and tires me out for the night. Faith has been to see me, bringing some apple slices and peppery watercress. Now she knows the foods that will not make me ill. Tired now is little me from all the climbing and sailing. Goodnight!

30th November

George came out into the garden after school, but I didn't see Faith. There is a large blue bouncer near my corner that is called Trampoline. George climbs up there and bounces away, not bothered by the fading daylight or the eerie darkness that follows. He jumps and jumps, sometimes landing on his knees and other times his bottom. George is completely fearless. When he injures himself he does not seem to care, but brushes the site of the hurt, seeming cross with it for interrupting his play. All of this while humming in his strange and tuneless voice.

Had he the wings, George would fly to the planets, I am sure of this.

1ˢᵗ December
Advent

It is December now, and Advent, so Faith tells me. I have never heard of advent before, but am looking forward to the daily gift that Faith will bring me to celebrate it. Today's was a carrot top with delicious fernery sprouting from the centre. Each day she receives a small present or chocolate for a 'calendar treat', and she promises to bring something for me.

I climb and jump, climb and jump, but still my wings are lifeless.

The rain is falling heavily now, a steady curtain of freezing grey that I feel sure will persist through the long dark night. It does not bother me. I find the steady drumming and splashing to be a very satisfying noise. There is a dip in the paving stones of this garden, under which lies the body of Faith's long dead cat, Roy. Water is collecting there at an alarming rate, and tonight I had a little swim in this puddle before settling down in my bed of sodden leaves. I am refreshed and cleansed, though perhaps I should have taken off my fur cape before the swim. It is taking some time to dry, and I fancy it will freeze tonight, stiff as a frost-gilded leaf! My stone belly is full from a lovely meal of burdock and ragwort, wonderful finds of my earlier foraging. Goodnight my invisible friend.

2ⁿᵈ December
Two Gifts

Two gifts on this very special day! One a skipping rope made out of string, beads threaded at each end for handles.

The second a new little person who has popped into my life. Her name is Dot and she emerged from the puddle. Such a wonder is Dot, an everlasting bubble of happiness! I cannot tell you more about her until I have told Faith. So many friends have I!

3rd December

Dot is her name, and so far as I can tell she is made from the water in the way that I am made from the stone, though puzzles like this do not trouble her at all. She just laughs and giggles away at my questions, popping into nothingness and then appearing somewhere else in an instant. A gorgeous face has she, chubby cheeks and eyes

as blue as the sky! Her hair is a mass of mesmerising, light-reflecting foam. I cannot see her at all in the water; which is the swimmer and which is the pool? Puzzles and more puzzles for my mind, but nothing bothers Dot. She calls me 'Bella' and I like it so. Faith says that she likes the name too, but can't get used to calling me it.

I dearly want Faith to meet Dot, but keeping my new little friend in one place long enough to arrange any kind of meeting is impossible. "Will you come back tomorrow?" I ask her earnestly, and she thinks a while, seeming to take my question seriously. Instead of an answer, though, she dips her dripping hand into the puddle and splashes me with icy drops. A delighted gurgling chuckle and then she is gone again. What fun; what confusion!

4th December
She comes and goes

Faith visits with the heavy, plodding regularity typical of humans. Humans do everything so slowly and steadily. They are comforted by routine. This is why they like indoors, I think. Tucked in their houses, they are slaves to neither weather nor season. They fashion their own seasons with the flicking of magical switches. Stacked up belongings and acquisitions anchor them to one place. It seems to me that humans fear the passage of time, so they cut each day up into sections and smaller sections, until every one is marked by a tick or a tock or a flashing bleep. In their ordered but confusing world, everything has a name and a place.

This is not the way of the outside world. Meeting with Dot has taught me this much. She can pop up in any place where water gathers. "What when the rain stops and the sun drinks up all the puddles?" I asked her in a growing panic. "What will you do?"

She laughs and laughs at me, troubled by nought.

"The water never dries up!" she told me, "it moves around. Up in the air, deep down underground. Puddles is not the end of things, Bella!"

I swim with her, though I am not nearly as fast in the water. She has wings an' all. I asked her if she can use them and she just laughed again, giving no explanation. What a merry little puzzle she is!

5th December

Today I awoke to a drip drip dripping on my little stone nose.

It was Dot of course, giddy with mischief. She said we should go for a ride upon a heavy black cloud that she had been sizing up, but I shook my head quickly.

"That cloud is so dense, a cow could ride upon it," she said as she looked heavenward. Something inside me wanted to take her sodden little hand and join in with her carefree adventuring, but my heart is more timid than hers. Easy for her, it is, popping up here and there, never a care in the world. She has never felt the shock of crumbling away and losing all of her memory and strength. Faith would understand, I am sure. I will chat with her tonight when she brings my advent gift.

Oh, and I have a gift for Faith! It is a stone semblance of her face which I fashioned from a pebble. Stone does as it's told, for me at least, so this modelling is easy. It looks so much like her! I think I will make one for Greta as well.

Not for Dot, though. She cares not for things. Not even clothes. She is a bubble as light as the air, and she will let nothing weigh her down.

6th December

I feel sad and directionless because Dot is gone. Who knows when or where she will next materialise? Perhaps she thinks me dull, and who can blame her? Little grey me, grubbing around in the leaves and the muck of the wall when she can float up into everywhere and anywhere without a single misgiving. How she brightens my life! We are opposites, her and I.

Faith knows what it is to worry. She has concerns about me all the time. Am I warm at night? Is my bed of leaves soft enough? What if the fox comes back, what if he is hungry?

She worries too about George; that he may never speak or lead a normal life. Now that we have been friends awhile, she feels able to share a few of these worries with me. While Faith is worrying, though, George is bouncing, humming and laughing. He falls and gets straight back up again without pausing to bother with pain or tears. I think it would be better for Faith to join in his fun today, and let tomorrow take care of itself.

With the dense, grey cloud hovering over us, Dot was completely unable to resist. She kept looking up and commenting on its dark edges backed by the silver winter sun; on the way its underbelly sagged, heavy and earth-bound.

"Come on, Bella, we're taking a trip," she said decisively.

I dint have time to decide a thing! She pulled me up, we skipped and floated on the air. I couldn't call it flying. Dot's hold on my hand was tight but wet, and as the earth stretched further and further away from my feet with each exhilarating breath, I felt her hold start to slip. Way above the ground I was now, so I looked up, not daring to look earthwards to where Faith's garden and my little pile of leaves were becoming smaller with each passing moment. Dot wasn't worried about the slipping grip. Dot wasn't worried about anything, so thrilled was she about the ever nearing grey mass of bouncy cloud.

I fell as only a stone can. Heavy and direct towards the earth. This would be the end of me for sure. The moment was everything and I scarcely tasted fear. How time slows down when the smashed and crumblesome end of you is imminent!

But here I am writing my journal, so dust I am surely not.

No, the blue net of Trampoline saved my fall, and a couple of little after- bounces later I realised that I was still one, not a hundred or a million little specks at all!

So Dot is gone, and Faith has yet to learn of my short, heavenward adventure. The dark is drawing in now, so I am sure she will be here soon.

7th December
Rat on the Loose

When Faith came out to visit me tonight her face was flushed pink and her eyes were smudged red with tears. Alby was gone. George had been in her bedroom, had opened the wire hatch of the rat's cage, and had not bothered to close it again. She was cross but not cross with him.

"He doesn't really understand," she told me, sadly. The sadness was not only about her missing pet, I think.

Immediate, I volunteered to help. Small as I am I can nose around in places where a big humanchild cannot.

"But Arabella, the inside world is so bad for you!" says she. I puffed up my stone chest and insisted that the cause was noble, and that it would take an hour at most to sniff out that good-hearted, smelly beast.

And I did it. I found him in the side cupboard! There is no light in there, only a thousand bags for 'Camping' or some such thing. Faith never would have found him, but I did, in less time than it takes for a wispy black cloud to cross the moon's haunted face. I came out riding on Alby's back, with my arms around his fat neck. I could have smelled him from the moon, believe me!

Faith gave Alby a treat of sausage, and for me, later on in the garden, tucked up and settled in my nest of leaves, slices of tomato and yellow pepper to go with the meal of fresh moss that I had collected. How delicious!

9th December
Becoming Arabella

Another special day. I am beginning to have what Faith calls 'Confidence'. At School, she tells me, she has a 'Confidence Class', where she is learning all about what it is to be a bold and brave person, about Body Language and Attitude and Positive Thinking. We have talked about it much, Faith and I. She says we are twin spirits and that we must learn together to walk out with courage into the Adventure of Life.

So today, under Faith's instruction, I did just this. I am missing Dot, and not quite sure that Faith believes in her, so I set about to find her for myself, instead of waiting for her little bubble of naughtiness to pop in my face.

Firstly, I went through the little wall where I spend an hour each day sleeping. It was easy as pie. Straight through I went, into another, completely different Garden. This Garden, Faith now tells me, belongs to 'Derek'. I have never seen Derek, but imagine him some kind of a king, with a beard, a golden sword and perhaps a jewelled crown. When I told this imagining to Faith she laughed, but would not tell me why.

In Derek's Garden there is a cage with two rodents, not quite like Alby the rat, but similar. I clambered over the wire fence, and was able to enter their home quite easily.

They are dear, these sweet ladies. I do not know their

names, and neither do they, it seems. Innocent beings indeed. One's fur is long and matted, bringing back a distant memory when I snuggled up to her. The other, more daring and inquisitive, is mostly brown but has a much shorter, shinier, coat. I spent some time with these rodents, they did not harm nor try too hard to befriend me.

Next I explored a waterfall with a brilliant sculpture and filled with pebbles that sparkled in the winter sunlight! I could imagine Dot popping up here, and just *knew* that she would do so any moment. She dint though.

Anyhow, news I had to tell Faith when she visited me tonight. I dare! I am a 'Dare Devil' (Or so Faith says). What will I dare do tomorrow? Read and you will discover.

Goodnight.

10th December
The Dare Devil Days

A strange feeling is this, knowing that you can do anything you want, but not quite having any ideas of where to start. I needed an adventure to tell when Faith paid me her evening visit, so I was determined to do summat!

I walked into the side of the wall that is Faith's house, not going *all* the way through, but finding myself tucked safely within the heart of its old, warm stones. Then I had an idea! I began to climb! Up and up, this is a very tall house. Swimming through tightly packed gravel is the only way that I can describe my journey. Up and up goes I, a slow and steady trek in the darkness of which I saw nothing but sensed the dizzying height. After what seemed like a whole night of gloom I pops out my head on the roof-tiles of Faith's house. High, high up was I. The tiles are shiny and smooth, and I walked across them with uncertain steps. To the attic window! I carefully looked in and there was Faith, home from school already, laid face down on her bed in her play clothes with her blazer and the rest of her school uniform strewn around her bedroom. Her bed was directly beneath, with only the cold glass of the window between it and me. She was as still as could be and I wondered if she was sleeping, until she stirred to turn the page of a book.

Right through the glass slips I! I have never travelled through glass before! So cold it was, like dipping in an icy puddle! I fell direct onto the bed where Faith lay, face down and reading.

She screamed and so did I! I don't know why! Then she stopped screaming, her own hand covering her mouth. Faith started to laugh and again, I copied her. We laughed so much! I explained about the upwards swimming through the bricks of her house. Shocked and amazed was my friend. It was not a journey I fancied re-tracing that night, so after an hour or so she slipped me into her fleece pocket and took me back outdoors to my familiar pile of leaves.

11th December

I have something important to tell you, invisible reader. You may think me even stranger than perhaps you did before. I will never know, but here it is. When I go into the stone wall of Faith's garden on an evening, I see little pictures. Little moving ghosts of memories that are so timid they vanish before I can properly examine them.

Sometimes the closeness of the stone feels like solid arms around me. Othertimes, I am sure that I hear a voice. It is a light, silvery voice that often calls my name. Then I feel the tug of my cape as Faith reminds me to come out of the stone depths, and when I try to remember the silvery words I cannot. I feel that my memories are silky shadows, insubstantial and ever slipping from my grasping hands.

12th December

I am writing by the light of the moon and stars. Such a clear night tonight, the air tastes fresh as icy water. I have seen Faith and George both, but there is still no sign of Dot. I long for her playful company but she is not in any place where I know to look. For a while tonight I waited at the fountain in Derek's garden (I saw Derek! He has white hair, brown skin and whistled a cheerful tune as he went about his garden business). I wonder, will, I ever hear Dot's tinkling bell laughter again?

13th December
Soft Snowflakes Fall

The first snow today! Tiny specks reflected the dazzling light of the sun. The wind chased them around in a flurry of cold and George and Faith came out to play. I had to stay back in the shadows for a while, though, as Faith's parents came out for a look too! The Father put on gloves and tried to scoop handfuls of the snow, but it was far too insubstantial and melted away at his touch. Faith's Mother stayed in the doorway frowning and drinking steaming tea from a cup.

All are gone now and I lay back on my soggy pile, letting the icy flakes fall into my open mouth.

14th December
A Comfortable Bed

Faith decided that she really needed to do something about my pile of leaves, which she said was both smelly and unsightly. How good she is to me! I hadn't noticed the smell at all, but now that she has scraped the soggy mass into a black bag with her father's garden trowel, and replaced the old leaves with fresh straw, I start to see what she meant!

The straw is fragrant and dry; I can burrow deep inside and breathe a smell that holds the promise of summer, or I can lie atop the bouncy bed counting the winter stars. Here I am now, happy and becoming sleepy. I closed my eyes a moment ago, but was awaked by a cold splat landing on my nose.

"Hello Bella!" said Dot.

15th December
Dot and the Falling Snow

My friend has returned to me as I felt sure that she would! How I have missed her! How exhausted she makes me feel after even a day of her company! But now the snow is falling more certainly. It began with small pinpoints of white, driven by the lively wind, first in one direction and then another. We danced with merriment, Dot and I, the whistling wind picking us up and dropping us every now and then. Dot tells me tales of the Snow Folk and says that we should go visiting with them. She says that these mysterious people are sure to welcome us. I am torn because here I have Faith, George, Greta and my comfortable pile of straw. I have the wall and all that lies beyond it. I have the rodents in Derek's garden and the friendly stars who watch over me.

Dot snorts at my sentiments.

"The stars are going nowhere," she says to me, "and anyway if you think that they are interested in your goings on then you are a stone fool. Come on, let's go adventuring!'"

Her excitement pulls me along like no other force. But I am a different creature entirely to her.

"Meet Faith with me, tonight, and we will talk to her together. She will want to know about these snow folk, I am sure, and she will feel happier of she knows where I am."

Dot will not be told though. She does not seem to hear ideas that do not please her. The tiny specks of snow grew fat in the twilight. Now they are falling like feathers and the world is becoming white. My tiny friend is stomping away, cracking ice on the puddle right now, and I have no indication as to whether she will stick around when Faith visits.

16th December
The World is White

Faith cannot come out, for she is ill with a Cold. She shouted from her parents' bedroom window before her Mother appeared behind her and the window was rudely slammed. I thought to travel through the stone of her walls and go to her, but I fear that her Mother is with her, tending her sickness. So that leaves me and Dot. Dot smiled when I told her that Faith would not be coming out, not sad at all for her illness.

The world that I have come to know is changing as each hour goes by. My pile of straw is a fluffy mound and the wall is gilded in sparkling crystals.

"The sky is packed with it," Dot said, looking up. An expert on the sky, she is.

"Then lets go visiting your Snow Folk" says I, all decisive. Guarded by her mother, Faith would not be venturing out into these icy conditions with her failing health, I was sure of that. We had nothing to lose.

17th December
Where are the Snow Folk?

Where are they, indeed? Made up for mischief, I shouldn't wonder. Dot trips and floats like a bubble on the snowy air. She takes my hand when I slow down, yanking me gently, urging me on. Her blue eyes sparkle and reflect no fear of the dazzling world.

Icicles hang in a row from a nearby rooftop, and Dot speculated today that this may be a good place to begin the search.

"Have you in fact met these folk before, Dot?" I asked her.

"Of course I've met them!" she said, indignantly. "Well, I've heard of them at least. I am sure I have heard of them. Or was it a dream?"

I caught a reflected glimpse of her face in the

shard of an icicle, and realised that she was teasing me. I sighed and followed, my frozen legs crunching through the carpet of white.

18ᵗʰ December

Either my jewelled book is becoming heavier, dear reader, or I am becoming weaker. I try to explain this to Dot. I cannot go for days and days without being inside the nourishing wall. She seems neither to understand nor to care. I can find nothing to eat in this wilderness of white and am cross with myself for such stupidity. Faith will be so worried. Will Dot take care of me if I become dizzy with weakness? She cares only for happy thoughts and does not trouble herself with the rest.

"Come *on*, Bella. I recognise this place," says she, squinting into the distance. I myself recognise nothing and feel blinded by the sheer expanse of white around me. Oh for a slice of cucumber or a fresh leaf of mint!

19ᵗʰ December
On and On We Go

Even Dot admitted that we must stop for a rest and some food. I suggested that we dig through the snow for moss but she giggled at this and said she would prefer Jelly and Ice-Cream. I do not know Jelly, and Ice does nothing for my appetite, so I dug for the moss myself. I found a sad and bedraggled clump and offered some to Dot, who declined and instead licked at some crunchy snow.

With our moods restored a little, it was ever onwards!

These snow folk (if they exist at all) are not the easiest of creatures to find.

20th December

The Snow Falls and we Rise!

Dot and I are cold to the core. Frozen solid she was this morning, an expression of pure annoyance on her chubby little face. I breathed and breathed on her until she could move again.

"This is not good, Dot,'" I told her, seriously.

"I know it! I cannot search on the ground, we will have to go to the clouds. It's much easier to see from up there."

'Oh no!" says I, remembering our last heavenward excursion.

"Oh yes!" my friend answered, grabbing my frozen arm before I had the chance to reason with her. Up and up we floated, this time with no Trampoline waiting to break our fall. I closed my eyes and waited for the end. The end did not come, so I opened them a crack. The world of pure whiteness stretched out beneath us like a soft blanket and strangely I felt safe. I looked up to where Dot was above me, her fleshy legs working frantically as though she were running on air. A heavy mass of cloud grew ever nearer and within moments we were upon it. Dot directed me to sit on the darkest, densest area, fearful to break her grip of me in case my heavy stone body slipped right through. It dint! I stayed right there, riding on the bouncy grey fluff above the beautiful winter world. The treetops and rooftops were clearly visible. A towering stone spire reached towards us, a spinning metal cockerel pinned cruelly to its tip.

As Dot and I looked at one another twin smiles transformed our faces into visions of glee!

21st December
Crys of The Snow Folk

It is bright blue above the clouds, like a summer's day with the heat turned off. Dot says that it is always this clear up here, although through the summer months the tops of the clouds are bathed in luxurious warmth.

Every step I took at first I fancied that it would be the plummeting end of me, but clouds are more substantial than you would think, or at least our cloud was! Dot ate a quantity of the fluffy stuff and became immediately fatter. I tried some too, but it was strange to me, like chewing steam. We played up there for some time, and I was beginning to wonder if Dot meant for us to come down at all, when a figure bathed in brilliant light arose from the depths of the billowing cloud.

"Ladies," he said with a bow.

"What is your name?" Dot asked, directly. There is no part of her that is shy in the least. Whatever she thinks will burst from her mouth in an instant.

"I am Crys," he said gallantly. Crys moved in a strange way, a million twitches stitched fluently together to form an otherworldly dance. Light was in and all around him, and his features were backed by an intricate web of blue that reflected light from the faraway sun.

"Take us to the Snow Folk then Crys," Dot demanded. "I have heard that they are throwing a party!"

"There is no need, my watery friend," Crys told her, with a kind smile. "The Snow Folk are on their way. I, indeed,

am the first of them. You will be our party guests."

Dot looked at me with a smug kind of a smile, and I returned it with a nervous and excited one.

Crys was so dazzling and beguiling to me that I felt I had to look away. I turned my head and looked downwards, towards the bouncing grey carpet of cloud. I closed my eyes to steady myself, but could not shake the vision of myriad geometry lighting his other-worldly face.

22nd December
A Party in the Clouds

The snow folk arrived in graceful ones and twos. They are so quiet and polite, these creatures, their names so unfamiliar but wonderful. 'Tryl' 'Lyze' and 'Miryall', twins who are called 'Shye' and 'Rhue', little ones that shine with an eerie blue light like the moon. 'Tylder' and 'Glyde'. They are breathtaking. Individually they are quiet and serene.

As more and more of the snow folk gathered on the grey, eerily lit stage, they stood in a circle, joined hands and from them issued a beautiful sound. At first I presumed that these creatures were singing, but that was not the case. The music came from within them, from the togetherness of them. I shall never forget the haunting, wordless sound of it, or the way that each note fell effortlessly into the next.

The music, and then the games! Games I have always thought are rough and playful, breathless occasions, but not the games of the snow folk. They float around, forming intricate patterns in the sky. Their movements are almost silent, laughter and joy coming from within and shining in their ghostly light. No one wins or loses these games; they are not a competitive people, I sense this. I feel that I am changed forever through my time with the snow folk.

23rd December

It has been some time since I ate a proper meal, and somehow Crys seemed to know this. As well, he knew the kind of food that I eat and was able to produce a plate of fresh greens and slices of wild, inky black mushroom. I ate greedily, and then lay back in the clouds for a rest.

"I believe you will soon need the comfort of your stones, Lady Arabella," he said to me softly.

"I am at home in the wall, but I love it here, Crys. I have never felt so relaxed. All of my anxiety has fallen away," I told him, sleepily.

"But do you have a family? Or a special someone who may be missing you?"

I sat up, and pulled my jewelled diary to me. Flicking through the pages, and taking note of the dates, I focused on the two words, 'Christmas Day'. I thought of Faith, and how much this day means to her. It was as though I could see the sadness on her face, and the image of her floated up through the translucent grey of the cloud, and then at once was unformed. She floated away from me in white, insubstantial wisps.

I looked at Crys, and he looked back at me, infinite understanding in his ice blue eyes.

"This cloud will not remain forever, Arabella. The party is nearly over. Perhaps time for you to go back down to earth."

"I do not know where Dot is. Dot brought me up here. And besides, I am so tired," I told him.

"Then sleep for the rest of the day" said Crys. He motioned to an area of the cloud, where appeared a foamy, mist-formed wall of stones. I smiled with wonder at his magic, and climbed wearily into the wall.

24th December
Snowflakes

It only seemed like seconds later that I was awake again, and the first face that I saw belonged to Crys. I feel like I have known him forever, his eyes are at once young and ancient, and his gentle manners make me feel both trusting and safe.

"Did you sleep well?" he asked me, a thousand expressions knitted into one.

"I think I did," I told him. The wall of cloud had now disappeared, as had most of the white, fluffy surface on which we stood. I noticed now that there were fewer snow folk around.

"And are you ready to return to your special someone?" Crys asked me.

"Yes please," says I, trusting that he would find a way to get me safely back down.

The remaining snow folk surrounded me, joining hands in a circle as they did. They began to make their unearthly sounds, moving around in a clockwise circle. I smiled at them, and they moved faster and faster around me. Soon I could not tell who was who; their faces seemed to merge into one. They had no faces! They were…snowflakes, each one different, each magically unique. The whirl of them went faster around and I was carried away on an icy wind with the heavenly sound of them surrounding me. Picked up bodily was I! Can you imagine how it felt for a little stone person to be carried off in this way, surrounded by

magic and light? The moments lasted forever, but at the same time were over all too soon. I awoke later upon my pile of straw. Dot was nowhere to be found.

25th December

Christmas Day at last! Faith does not know that I am back, so I decided to surprise her. I dare not walk through the stone walls of her house into the downstairs rooms, as I am not sure who may be there and what they may make of me. So I climbed. Up and up through the rubble of the bricks, a familiar path. Attic-wards swam I, towards Faith's uppermost room. It was very early in the morning when I started this journey, the birds had not yet started to make their daybreak sounds not had the light of the sun begun to illuminate the eastern horizon. Up and up goes Arabella Crumblestone, breathing in the particles that Faith's house is made of. I felt strong and alive, absorbing the ancient goodness of the stone.

Through the chill of the glass pane goes me, calculating the drop so I would land directly on the soft bed belonging to my 'special someone'! I fell, I landed, I bounced, but she was not there! Her room was littered with crumples of brightly patterned paper, but no Faith and no George neither. Alby sat fatly in his cage, watching me with his beady black eyes. I approached and leaned against the bars,

"Where is she, Alby?" I asked, but of course, he did not reply.

I spent the day in Faith's attic room, looking for clues as to her whereabouts. When eventually I heard footfalls on the wooden stairs, I sprinted to the safety of Dolls' House, where I watched from the gap of the window to see who the steps belonged to, though in my stone heart, I already knew.

Faith, my friend beneath an armful of boxes.

I tumbled from the window of Dolls' House and ran to greet her, shouting her name.

She dropped the boxes and scooped me up. When I looked into the depths of her green eyes I saw welling tears.

"Happy Christmas," I said, kissing the side of her nose.

26th December
I Am Changed

I am changed for good, and Faith sensed this within moments of our reunion. Confidence, she says, is not something that can truly be learned in class. I have spoken to her in a hushed voice of my adventure in the clouds, of Crys (who she believes that I Love, and now that she has said so, I believe so too). I talked to her of my growing certainty that I can survive without the wall, indeed, without all of the things that I once thought were my Life. But that I can come back to this life and to those very things that I love, and they may still be here, and I can love them all over again.

I have no Christmas gift for Faith but this wisdom. She says quietly that it is enough.

Goodnight.

27th December
Back to the wall

After spending an exhausted two days and nights in Faith's room, we both felt that it would be wise for me to return to the outside elements that are my natural home. I have slept for two hours inside the wall this evening, from the time when the light of day begins to drain away and a chill claims the evening air. I feel thoroughly well as I look to the friendly stars, and the wisps of dark cloud that separate me from them. *I have been there*, thinks I, amazed. Not to the stars, you understand, but why not? What is stopping me? Nothing has ever stopped me but my crippling fears, and now they have drained away, melted along with the snow of yesterday. I drink in the night's peace as I stretch out upon my pile of straw.

28th December

Whatever Faith wants to do, then I will do it with her; this was the thought that I awoke with today. She is still holidaying from school for Christmas, even though Christmas is gone. So happy was I to see Greta and George. They were all out bouncing on Trampoline, wrapped up warmly in Anoraks and Gloves. Faith told me that they were going out to dinner and *I* asked *her* to be slipped into the silken pocket of her Anorak and included in the dining. The restaurant was too warm for me, but I was not afraid. Faith slipped me a slice of tomato, and when my friends went outside to play on the climbing frame, I emerged happily from her Anorak pocket to gulp the fresh winter air. Greta placed me halfway down a silver slide and watched me go speeding to the end before Faith caught me in her two-cupped hands. Here I am back home, wishing on the midnight stars that someday I will see Crys again.

29th December

In the mirror of Dolls' House today, I noticed how ragged and bedraggled I looked.

"No!" said Faith, my faithful Faith, "you are the most beautiful thing in the whole world." I smiled warmly at her, for I could sense that she believed such nonsense.

"But look!" says I, spinning around in a circle so that she could assess the tears and stains and the hanging threads of my garments. My cape of fur is now tangled with old leaves and mud; sodden and dried, sodden and dried so many times that the fur is fur no more, shiny clumps with all kinds of pieces of nature woven in for good measure.

Faith is going to Shopping tomorrow with her Mother and Greta. She says that she will buy materials to make new garments for me. She says that she will Style me! I can hardly wait. To be dressed in colours of the rainbow, reflecting the happiness of my heart. I told Faith that I would be happy to come along to Shopping with her, that I would hide quietly in the dark, secret depths of her pocket and only peek out when she signalled that it was safe. Faith said that this was too risky. I made a big-eyed begging face but still she said no. I am happy though. Yes, very happy today.

30th December
A New Year; A New Arabella

The New Year is nearly upon us and I will be dressed for adventure as well as beauty. Faith laid out all of the fabrics on her bed for me to pick favourites. I will have playing and adventuring clothes, I will have party clothes ("Yes, Faith, I *do* go to parties," I told her), I will have clothes for every occasion. Faith will keep these for me on a rail in Dolls' House, and if her mother becomes suspicious, she will tell her that she has made them for the animal figures that she keeps there. There is fabric of silken green, fluffy white fur, pliable brown leather and all manner of sequins and tiny stones. We ate together up in Faith's room; cheese on toast for her and yellow pepper slices for me, with slurps of cool apple juice to wash it down. Later in the garden, a little sleep in my comforting wall before my friend tugged the ragged edges of my cape and out I came.

Excitement and calm wash over me in beautiful cool waves. It is dark now, and a light, refreshing rain is falling. Dot is near. Ask me not how, but I can sense her. I will not call out to her, though, I will let her think that she has surprised me. Ah, here she is now, flicking water at me from the guttering. I shall cover my diary with straw, and go out to play.

31st December

Dot does not understand why the making of my new wardrobe is causing such a stir. I tried to tempt her into meeting Faith with the promise of a shawl or shiny swimming suit, but she shrugged in her carefree way.

"Why don't your raggy wings work, anyway?" she asked me.

A good question is that. I told her that they were just for decoration and she laughed till her belly jiggled. Of course, I understand the joke. Decorative my useless wings most certainly are not. I laughed along with her to show her that I didn't care, and then she pulled me up to Trampoline where we both had a happy time bouncing as high as we could. Lights flickering on in the house warned us that the adults could be near, so off we skipped, into Derek's garden where I thought to show Dot the fountain. Surprise surprise, she already knew about it.

I only saw Faith for a few minutes today, she was going on a Visit to her grandfather's house. She promises me more of her time tomorrow. Goodnight.

1st January

I stayed awake the whole of last night watching explosions of colour and sparks that filled the night sky. Oh, Faith forgot to tell me! "Fireworks" she says they are, lit to make Celebration. The first bang scared me into wakefulness, and then the colours tempted me from my bed of straw. Dot lay back in a puddle looking up in wonder, with the explosions of colour reflected in the clear water of her big, round eyes. Of course, she has seen these lights many times, but could not tell me the details of their name or purpose. She supposed they were animals, or faeries of some type, dancing in the manner of the Snow Folk. I believed this throughout the night, and my mind throbbed with the enigma of it. No, "Fireworks" Faith tells me today. I believe Faith.

2nd January
Arabella Crumblestone is Waking Up

Though my ragged wings may not work, I feel that there is much more to me. There is a fizzing within me and I sense things; like the nearness of Dot, or a trouble in the life of my dearest Faith. I felt something wrong this morning, something strangely amiss. The beady, cold eye of the sun was high in the busy, cloud-strewn sky, peering down on the world's goings on, but interfering in nothing.

I was sitting idly atop the rodent's cage in Derek's garden when I felt a need to be near the House. Through the wall comes I, practiced now, and quicker than you would believe possible. George was in the garden, busily emptying out the contents of a small cardboard box onto the stone flags. Tiny twigs with red ends spilled out all over the place. I watched carefully as George picked up these twigs, and let them fall back to the ground, over and over again. These repeated activities often engage him for long periods of time. Indeed, I watched on for what seemed like an age until he became bored and started to stamp on the twigs, rubbing them against the stone flags with the soles of his big brown boots.

I tasted wisps of pungent Smoke, and I ran to where George was stamping. I put aside my fear of being crushed, so determined was I to distract him from this dangerous activity. Though George says no words, I feel that he understands quite a few.

"No!" I shouts up at him, hands on my hips.

He stopped his stamping immediately and looked down to where I was. He stooped to pick me up, and there was I, trapped in his big hand, with the red tipped twigs a forgotten jumble on the stones.

He carried me inside, through the glass doors. All the while I repeated calmly "Put me down, George. Be a good boy and put me down," but in his sturdy grip I remained. The skin of his hand was rough and chewed in places and I stroked it's dry, cracked surface with my small stone fingers. Faith came into the dining room and I shouted to her as loudly as I could "George has me, Faith!"

I am unhurt, and mostly the twigs (Match Sticks, Faith says) are cleared away, safely in the box of card and stashed behind the locked Kitchen door.

I found a stray one tonight, though. It had rolled between the gap in the paving stones, and I was able to gently prise it out of the mossy crack. Being too late to tell Faith about the single Match, I have hidden it away in my pile of straw.

Faith says I am a Hero and could have saved all of their lives. I don't know about Hero. I don't really know what I am.

3rd January

My clothes are ready. Faith brought me safely up to her attic room where they were laid out ceremoniously on her bed. Such clothes! With the green silk she has fashioned a beautiful gown for me, with lacy straps at the shoulders and a matching cape. Sparkling sequins at the waist make the whole ensemble look quite breathtaking. She has tried very hard to keep her stitches small, but as I am so much tinier than she, I can see them quite clearly, like small, even teeth nibbling at the edges of my garments.

There is a tunic of soft leather with a belt containing a tiny silver sword that Faith has borrowed from an Ornament. I have a sword! And a peaked hat of leather to wear instead of my rose-thorn crown. I was unsure at first. I love the hat, but have grown used to my crown. Faith says not to worry, and that it is good to have Choice. Well yes; thanks to Faith, I now have a choice. What I have chosen today, because of the freezing temperatures and a rising desire for adventure, is a long trouser suit in autumn green, my sheathed sword at my hip and my cap of leather upon my head; trails of hair all tucked up inside it.

Let the adventure of life commence!

4th January

Last night after my diary writings I was so restless. So longing, but for what I could not rightly say. I felt someone close by and knew that it was not Dot. No, it was a different someone. In a trance of excitement I took the Match-Stick from beneath my bed of straw and dragged it along the rough surface of the stone flag. Dark smoke curled and stretched through the living night air, and then a crackle, a spark – a flame. That someone I sensed needed the flame to jump into being, I felt this with all of my stone senses. I dragged a handful of my straw bed away from the pile, and let it rest at the flaming head of Match-Stick. Oh foolish Arabella (I hear you say it!) performing the exact deed that I had distracted George from just two days previous. I encouraged a little fire that was soon crackling with energy. I sat; I waited, ensuring that no tinder could lead the flames from the fire's heart to my comfortable bed.

I did not wait long before from the core of the flame leapt a being, blue at the centre, orange at the edges and surrounded by a wobbling energy. He fixed his flaming eyes on me for some moments before either of us thought to speak.

"Are you a fire faerie?" I asked of the stranger.

He shook his head, though looked puzzled and lacked conviction.

"Where am I?" he asked, all a-daze.

"You are in the Garden of Faith Raymondson, and in the company of Arabella Crumblestone. I made the fire from which you stepped. Do you know your name, at least?" I asked.

"Blaize?" he ventured, his crackling voice lacking surety. "I am Blaize." He did not hold out his hand for me to shake, and for this I was glad. What would a touch from such a hand do to me?

The small fire had now burned itself out and was just a pungently smoking pile of ash. Blaize looked from it to me, and then back at it once more before leaping off into the dark night.

5th January
I Do Not Recognise Myself

I have spent the past few hours looking back upon the pages of this journal, and it is true to say that I do not recognise the timid creature that first began these writings. I am Arabella Crumblestone! I have many powers, my invisible friend, and these are emerging day by day. My memories are also coming back to me, and - it makes me shiver right through to think that I could have ever forgotten this fact - I have a Mother. I remember her, though the memory is hazy, like that of a dream character. Mother's arms. The silken nature of her voice. The warmth of her holding me tightly. The knowledge that she would always put things right for me.

What happened for me to leave her? Is she still out there somewhere?

And yet another puzzle - I have unleashed a fire faerie into this world; the world that I love. The world that my dear Faith and Dot and Crys inhabit. I have unleashed this fire and I am not afraid, for I sense the same timidity in Blaize that was once in me. I feel sure that Blaize means no harm. I must find him, though. I must also find Mother, wherever she may be.

I searched the land around Faith's garden for clues to help me answer my many questions, and have found a Blackbird with an injured wing. She fears me. Among all of the other concerns, the one at the forefront of my mind is how to help this Blackbird to heal without scaring her half to death. Her wing is bent awkwardly and I see that she is in pain, thirsty and hungry. When Faith comes out into the garden later on I will speak with her about this most imminent of my problems.

6th January
Blackwing

I call her Blackwing. I have gained a little of her trust and shared the secret of her with Faith, who refuses to come too near, worried that the sight of a human girl such as herself will be the failing of Blackwing's fragile heart. Faith says that I must guard Blackwing vigilantly as she would be easy prey for any stray cat or hungry fox. I have hunted for the first time, piercing the flesh of a fat worm with my silver sword. Slices of the worm I put in reach of Blackwing, though I spared Faith this grisly fact. The nourishment of wormflesh brought a glint to the blackbird's eye, and after she had eaten I spliced her wing with a Toothpick and cotton that Faith brought for me. I do not know how I have the knowledge to complete this task, but I was confident in my doctoring, my hands nimble and steady. It seems that the more that is required of me, the more I can give.

Dot called and asked me to come playing, but I cannot leave Blackwing's side, and could find no joy in play until the bird is healed. My friend went quickly and haughtily off, her wet wings flipping with displeasure, but what else could I do?

I shall hunt again in the early hours of tomorrow morning, when I have successfully guarded my patient through the risky hours of the night.

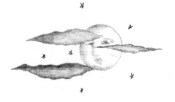

7th January

I have time for little else but the bird's care. Last night I caught three bugs with my silver sword (how timely that Faith gave it to me when she did.) I found a bird's voice deep within my throat, and trilled sounds of comfort to Blackwing. She looked up and seemed to recognise the sound. I heard a rustling in the hedgerow and was prepared to defend her against hawk, fox or feral cat. No creature came though. Blackwing will live, of this I am determined. Most of all she needed water, which Faith brought in a tiny glass bottle. I emptied a little at a time into the lid, and placed this close to Blackwing's beak. Despite her pain and fear she had the courage to stoop and to drink. I trilled the comforting bird's song to her again. She *will* survive.

8th January
The Smell of Flame

The silver eyed fox came back, perhaps smelling Blackwing's vulnerability. I was ready with my sword, but in reality, to a fox, a jab from it would be but an annoyance in the scraggly red fur.

The heady smell of fox was so near, and I was unsure as to how I could keep the vagabond from swallowing Blackwing in one greedy gulp. Why had I not asked Faith to find me some kind of cage or large box for her, so to provide at least a little protection? But no, the old Arabella may have spent hours pondering this question, but the new brave Huntress with her silver sword paced up and down, swaying her weapon, daring the fox to pounce.

With a crackle and a flash that I was not expecting at all, a flaming figure fell from the foliage above. Blaize! The newly emerged fire faerie. Our eyes met, mine defiant and battle-ready, his filled with flickering doubt. I understood in an instant his good intentions. I gathered some dried twigs and grasses, and he lit them, with a sweep of his burning hand so that an acrid black smoke issued from the pile. The fox, still hidden in the undergrowth, slunk back and was gone in moments. Blackwing, of course, was panicked by the smells of fire and fox, her injured wing twitching and dark eyes cloudy with pain. I went to her, cooing softly as I stroked the downy feathers on her head.

When I turned to thank Blaize for his intervention, he was gone again. The only trace of him was a black, smoking patch in the undergrowth.

9th January

It seems that Blaize has a good, if very serious soul. He has only ever uttered a handful of words to me yet I feel I know so much of his personality. Deeds speak so much more than words, as I am learning.

Faith visited me today with grains for Blackwing and radish tops for me. I ate the radish tops and some of Blackwing's grains, before asking Faith to bring yet more food. This hunting and guarding and never resting leaves me hungry all of the time. Two black bugs were impaled on my silver sword today. I watched impartially as the twelve legs twitched and ran towards nothing but death, and once they were still, fed the bugs to Blackwing, who seems to be gaining in strength if not in humour. She trembles when I venture near, and does not respond well to my touch.

Faith told me that a watery little being popped up in her bath last night. Dot! That funny little faerie. Probably she is bored with me being in no mood for games these days, with all my energy being used to return Blackwing to a state of health. I can not let her die. I will be a Mother to her.

10th January

It is so hard! The sun has risen six times since I first found my injured friend and pledged to see her well again. I am finding that to care this much for another is gravely hard work. It is a preoccupation of my mind how hard a mother must toil to ensure her offspring's survival. Diligence. Work until you are exhausted and then work and work some more. And if the seductive voice of sleep calls sweetly in the night? Ignore this voice and work on! Blackwing allowed her head to rest upon my shoulder today, so I will take that as proof of her trust. Another fat worm, more grains from Faith. My belly rumbles and craves more substantial food than the watery cress and mushrooms that I am used to. Faith brought bread with butter, and I gobbled it greedily. She brought cold tea in a bottle, and I drank this down in one. She is worried for me but knows that I will never be dissuaded from my task. Dot, showing uncharacteristic wisdom (or perhaps just peeved at my distraction), has not tried to tempt me to play in puddle nor fountain today. I have seen nought of Blaize, and have barely had time to think of Crys or the other Snowfolk. The snow has gone now, anyway, and may not be back for another year. Blackwing occupies most of my thoughts, and this is a good thing. Bringing her slowly back to health stops me from pondering deeper, more shocking matters. I pour all of my strength into being a good mother.

11th January

Faith came tonight with Milk that she had thought for Blackwing, but smelling the creamy drink, I instinctively knew it wrong for her. I gulped it down, so Faith's efforts were not in vain. It filled every part of my stone being with energy, and I stretched in the Winter sun and felt the glory of life. Yes, you have guessed! Blackwing is recovering. She can now move her wing freely and with no pain.

Faith has looked into a Library Book and discovered that mending a bird's wing is one of the most difficult tasks ever to be successfully achieved. A Professional Human, who may have worked with animal and bird for thirty years, will struggle to achieve this feat. I think of human hands now, of the size and clumsiness of them, and am not surprised that my tiny fingers could have performed this operation with more accuracy.

Blackwing's eyes are now clear as berries, and her appetite has returned with a vengeance.

This means more and more hunting for Arabella Crumblestone. So hungry was I tonight that I thought to taste a slice of wormflesh, but on seeing the freed half of my victim squiggle away into an earthy sanctuary my appetite was momentarily crushed.

So tired am I, that if Blaize, Crys, or even Dot happened to drop by I would gladly sleep for an hour whilst they guarded the injured bird. But for the friendly stars I am alone. My twinkling guardians seem distant tonight though, and, through the exhausted lens of my vision, they merge into one undulating light.

12th January
A Helping Hand

Dot placed her hands on her hips, and paced up and down crossly.

"Dusty wings, see, Bella. A bird don't fly with dusty wings. Unnatural, that is."

"And what do you suggest, Dot?" I asked her.

"Well, a little birdy bath, o'course," she said, matter-of-factly. She busied herself searching around the garden and eventually unearthed a half-buried plant pot. This she dragged over to where Blackwing and I were hiding out, plonking it down in front of us with a happy 'clever-me' kind of a smile.

"Well that really is wonderful," I said with a little laugh, "but there's no water in there!"

"Ha!" Dot said simply. She held her hand over the brown pot, and water streamed in from her fingers. She diminished in size quite considerably as the water flowed from her, and while I was at first amazed at her powers, I very quickly became alarmed, fearing that she would melt wholly away.

"Dot! That's enough!" says I, standing up and reaching out to her rapidly shrinking frame.

"Well, now she's worried about me an' all!" Dot told Blackwing, a little unkindly. "Don't worry, Bella, I'm off for a long drink in the fountain. You get this scruffy bundle of feathers washed! It'll cheer her up no end."

Well, my silly friend has wisdom in her soul after all! I splashed the water onto Blackwing's feathers, rubbing and stroking until they shone with an eerie blue sheen in the morning sun. Blackwing helped with her grooming, holding water in her yellow beak and splashing it over her feathers.

After her bath she opened and closed her wings a few times in order to dry them.

Clever Dot indeed! Once Blackwing is fully mended I will pay her more attention, I promise this.

13th January
Prowling Fox

With help first from Blaize, then Dot, and frequent gifts of seeds and nuts from Faith, I was beginning to feel that my task was nearly done, and that any day now Blackwing would rise to the sky, all magnificent and proud, and once again I would be free to play and bounce and explore the world.

But the fox is back. I have not seen him but I know that he is there, his rustlings are faint and stealthy in the undergrowth. I know it is him, though do not ask me how. Tonight, again, I will not sleep at all. I write now by the light of the moon. Blackwing is gently resting and the sounds of the night are all around us. Wish me luck, invisible reader. I shall need it!

14th January

All last night I paced with my silver sword, guarding the sleeping Blackwing. I spoke with my mind to the midnight prowler: *I know where you are fox. I am an excellent swordswoman. Do not come near us. A dalliance with my silver weapon could be the end of you, my friend.* The words were pure fear dipped in a coating of bravery.

Whether the fox understood my thought-words, or smelled the unusual nature of my powers, I cannot be sure, but he kept to the undergrowth, or maybe found some other unfortunate to feast upon. It is morning time now and so tired am I. Blackwing has grown accustomed to trusting me, and so I shall curl up next to her, taking comfort in her warmth and in the rhythmic lullaby of her beating heart.

15th January
Test Flight

From the moment Blackwing opened her shining eyes early this morning it was clear to me that she was well again. There was a spark in her eyes, a knowing glint of pure pleasure. A bird cannot smile, of course, what with the rigidity of its beak, but her eyes conveyed an ocean of love.

I stood back and watched as she trotted along the straw-strewn garden, hopping quickly up onto the low stone wall. It was hard for me to stay still, watching this miracle unfold. When you are used to caring for someone or something, it is strange to stand back and watch them go on alone. But hop up she did, and stretched her blue-black wings. One flap, then two, and before I had time to issue a quick prayer or wish, off she went. Up and up, not turning even for a goodbye glance.

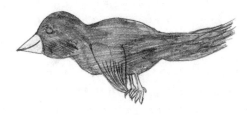

I was glad. Of course I was glad. Feelings of gladness and sadness were smudged together. I smiled and cried and before the tear had dripped down the end of my stone nose, she was back again, with a wriggling worm as a gift for me! Of course, I did not want it, but was glad of the gesture. I pointed my silver sword towards it and she gobbled it down.

I went to go and hug my cured patient, and my arms were securely around her neck in a fond embrace. She misunderstood, and took off again, with me dangling precariously from her like an ungainly necklace.

"*Blackwing!*" says I, my breath left behind. I scrambled my legs over her back and we flew, soaring into the morning sky! The trust that she had given to me over the past few days I shared in her too, and once my breath had returned to me I whooped with the glory of flight!

16th January
My Efforts Have Bound Her To Me

Blackwing will not leave me. Of course, this is a wonderful thing, but I dearly want for her to have a natural life, to find a mate and have a nestful of hatchlings. She will not go at all and hovers around Faith's garden day and night. I have tamed her with my healing! Dot fancies her some kind of flying slave, to take us to this party, or that lake, but no. Blackwing should revert to being a wild bird. Perhaps I will have to ignore her attentions until she has forgotten me.

17th January
Wriggling Worms

Faith and I went up to her attic room today; my dear friend has made me yet more clothes, before I have even had the chance to wear many of the other garments. A brown woollen coat with toggles, matching scarf and hat. Three pairs of tiny socks to keep my stone feet warm (a master is Faith at the art of Knitting), a colourful Poncho (I love this! I am wearing it now!) and a tiny knot of silken roses to wear in my hair. So good to me is Faith. We were doing a Fashion Parade, where I tried on all of the garments, walking up and down as though through crowds of cheering on-lookers, when we heard a tap-tapping on the attic window. We both looked up at once to see Blackwing staring in, her beady eye bright and glinting. In her mouth was a wriggling brown worm, another present for me!

"Blackwing is determined for you to have a worm, Arabella," Faith said through her giggles. The worm was unceremoniously dropped onto the flat window, where it wriggled and turned and turned and wriggled.

Faith told me that, as a special treat, her mother would be taking her and Greta to the Cinema to see a Moving Film tomorrow night. She asked me if I would come along too. Only moments after Faith had asked me what I thought of this plan, Dot plopped up from Faith's glass of water and said cheekily, "Can I come?" Faith and I laughed some more and Dot joined in, although I don't know if she got the joke. I am not sure that I did either, but it felt so good with the three of us together at last, laughing on and on. In the end Faith agreed that Dot could come too. The moving film is called Alice in Wonderland, a *classic,* Faith says.

18th January
Wonderland

Dot did not come with us in the end. She was appalled by the idea of having to hide in Greta's pocket until we got into the Screen Room. She folded her arms, shook her foamy head stubbornly and said that she would meet us there.

"Have you any idea how to get to Cineworld, Dot?" I asked her.

"I can get anywhere where there's water. I'm sure there is water at this Cineworld. Hmm?" Dot directed this question towards Faith, who looked from her to me and to Greta before saying,

"Actually, Dot, I don't think that there is any water there. We could take some in a bottle, if that would help?"

"Ok, but make sure there's no lid, will you? I don't want to be no genie in a bottle, for definite!"

And so it was agreed that she would meet us there, to avoid the dark depths of Greta's coat pocket. I don't mind travelling by pocket. Not at all. I bounce and jig along, feeling the hum of the car journey, or the gentle rocking to and fro as Faith walks along. Faith's Mother said goodbye in the car park of Cineworld, as she was on her way to Shopping, I listened to the sometimes rich and sometimes shrill tones of her voice as she told Greta and Faith what time she would collect them.

When Faith told me that it was safe, I peeped my little head out into the magical world of the Cinema for the first time ever! No Dot was here to be found. A little worried I was about this at first, especially since we seemed to have forgotten all about the bottle of water. How cross my little friend would be!

But when the magical pictures started to move across the giant screen, I became so engrossed in the story of Alice with her shrinking and growing, her endless chasing of the White Rabbit, and the smiling, smiling Cheshire Cat, that I forgot all about Dot and the water and how cross she might be.

I was soon reminded, though, when up she popped in Faith's sparkly orange drink.

"I'm all sticky!" says she, most horrified.

The three of us, Greta, Faith and I, looked at Dot in amazement. Not only was she all sticky, but she was coloured a most shocking shade of orange!

We giggled so much that people from the row in front

turned to tell us to be quiet. Fortunately, because of the darkness, I wasn't spotted, and neither was the sticky, fluorescent Dot!

As Dot and I bathed in Derek's fountain later on that night, and the colour ran out of her, we talked about the human world, the wonder world, Cineworld, and how none of these were really *our* world.

"We need to find our own kind, you and I. There must be more of me, and I know there's more of you 'cause I've seen them."

"*What*?" I asked and asked of Dot to tell me more, but in her own infuriating way she refused, changing the subject, making it into a joke, and in the end disappearing completely in a cascade of bubbles.

A clear night it is tonight. I look up to the stars and offer my stone heart full of wishes to them. The stars shine and shine, but they have no answers to give.

19th January

Tonight I watched from my pile of straw as George bounced and bounced on Trampoline. I would like to have joined him, so much fun we could have the two of us. I trust him, I think. He definite means no harm. Of course, a big boy like this should talk, but he neither talks nor shows any desire to. Here is another problem for me to contemplate as I polish my silver sword.

Blackwing hovers constantly, bringing me her little 'treats', bugs, plump winter berries, and more worms. Of course I do not want the bugs nor the worms neither, but a tasty berry will never go amiss in Arabella Crumblestone's belly.

I embraced Blackwing in a thank you and she waited patiently for me to climb on. Off we took, Trampoline, Faith's house and the patchwork of gardens becoming a tiny picture of themselves amid the rest of the scenery. We enjoyed the dusky night air, Blackwing and I, as we swooped and dived, with the black silhouettes of the trees forming a lacy web against the colourful sunset.

And now here I am back at my pile, counting my questions on the stars that grace the endless midnight sky.

20th January
Love and Swimming

"Love? You cannot love him if you forgot all about him. What is the point of love anyway? Silly load of slush, you Pebble!"

Dot, of course, was talking of Crys. Another flurry of

snowfall had brought his memory whirling back into my conscious mind. Memory was all though, for there was no sign of Crys nor the other Snow Folk. What is wrong with me? No matter what I have in my life it seems that I always crave more. My heart is a skittering little butterfly flying from one thing to the next, never staying in one place long enough to fully belong.

"You may be right," I said to Dot, sadly, and then, to cheer us both up, "shall we go swimming in the fountain?"

"I know a better place to swim," Dot told me, mysteriously. "You'll have to call Blackwing. She can take us."

"Blackwing is not our servant, Dot," I told her again, but on the mention of her name, the blackbird instantly swooped, causing a large black shadow to hover over us in the twilight.

"Maybe you should tell her that," said Dot. Blackwing allowed us both to climb aboard her back, and my little friend directed her to a beautifully starlit lake where we swam for what seemed like hours until the ghost of the pale moon faded into the new day's sky.

21st January
The Snow Comes and Goes

I spent my nourishing hour within the depths of the wall today, and ate cress and lettuce leaves which Faith smuggled out in her pocket.

The snow comes and goes causing little flurries of excitement both in my heart and in the world at large. The flakes are soft, but can quickly be whipped up into a frenzy by the excitable wind. Dot is staying so close to me these days, I think unnerved by all the time I spent away from her while nursing Blackwing.

Blackwing, too, is never far away. As often as I refuse the worms and grubs that she brings for me, she still brings more. The joke is wearing thin but Dot laughs on.

I feel that Dot is planning something, and I watched on as she studied the sky.

"What will the weather do, Dot?" I asked, silently wishing for snow. She shrugged, though, and changed the subject.

I am Alice, chasing and chasing a white rabbit that will always be three steps ahead.

22nd January
Dreaming

Have you ever dreamed a dream so vivid and real that you were unsure as to which was the dream and which the reality? This happened to me last night; or perhaps it was this morning. I usually sleep so lightly, wakened by any owl hoot or rustle from the undergrowth. Last night, though, sleep enveloped me like a heavy blanket, wrapped all around, under and over.

I heard her calling me at first, and within the dream I was within the wall. I was fighting to get out, but had to rely on Faith to tug at the corner of my poncho. I waited and waited for the tug, but Faith was not there and I had to scramble through the rubble, breathing in the ancient powdery dust, which half blinded me in my panic.

My mother's voice was calling.

It was not a call that I could have ignored, sleeping, wakeful, or curled up in a wall within my dream.

"I'm here!" I tried to shout to her, but my mouth was

full of crumbling stone.

"Arabella, Arabella. Time to come home!"

I was swimming far too long through the stone, which became bouncy white cloud. Crys was there, his myriad eyes filled with endless wisdom. I tried to tell him that my mother was calling me, but no words would issue from my stone mouth. I felt that he understood anyway, I felt that he could help me find the way, but then Dot bobbed up from the buoyant foam of the cloud, dragging me under and down down down back to the starlit lake where there was no one but us.

And now I am here, wakened, in my fragrant pile of straw, and the sun has risen high in the sky and Blackwing hovers over, perhaps fearing that I am ill.

"Ah, thank you, Blackwing." She has another worm for me, to aid my recovery, no doubt.

23rd January
Embers

It has been a lovely day, bright, cheerful and bitterly cold. The cold does not bother me, though, only in that Faith cannot spend too long outside. I am happy to go up to her room for an hour in the evening, to chat and to lay on the dubious comfort of the Dolls' House bed.

My outdoor clothes are my favourite, with the poncho atop for colour and flair. Up in Faith's bedroom, however, I wore the gown that she has sewn for me. Looking at myself in the smoky mirror of Dolls' House, with my vibrant green hair cascading around my shoulders like a mossy waterfall, I could not help but wonder what Crys would make of me in this attire. I shall not know, though, for although the snow comes and goes, Crys remains a snow white memory, distant but fond.

Tonight I sensed a glowing presence beyond the wall. I swam through the rubble of it to Derek's garden, whereupon I found Blaize, or more true to speak, what was left of Blaize. The flaring beacon of a faerie that I had released from the Match Stick had diminished considerably since our last meeting, when he had used his living flame to hold back the hungry fox. Now he was but a smouldering ember.

"Oh Blaize," the words fell from my frightened lips.

He looked up from where he was slumped on the dewy grass. His once orange eyes were dull and dark, and there seemed to be no strength about him at all.

I went to him at once, throwing my stone arms around him. He seemed to come undone in my embrace, smouldering parts of him falling away to dust and then nothingness. This could not be. Brave and frightened

Blaize! I must help him. But how? Surely Crys would know. But Crys was in some other place and here was I with a crumbling, smouldering friend and a rising panic in my heart.

I stopped and breathed the night air, knowing that fretful actions would do nothing to aid this dire situation.

I looked up to the stars, twinkling away in their velvet eternity. I closed my eyes to steady myself. Sounds, sights and smells fell away as the world slowed down. I held on to Blaize's cooling hand, and a sudden warmth passed between us.

"Fan the flames, Arabella," said a silken voice in my mind.

Thank you, Mother.

On opening my eyes, I saw that Blackwing had descended from a nearby Sycamore. She watched in silence as I waved my stone arms rhythmically, causing the glowing embers that were my friend to brighten and spark. And then Blackwing was by my side, flapping her magnificent wings, causing a breeze that I could have not have even hoped to with my thin little arms. Within moments, Blaize was blazing once more. Blackwing stopped her fanning and cocked her head to one side, as though examining her work.

24th January

Soon after Blackwing and I had fanned him back to his flaming former self, Blaize fled again. I sat back, exhausted from the fanning, and his orange light disappeared into the foliage.

"Blaize, wait," I called out to him.

For some reason he is afraid and constantly running. If I were to lose him again, how on earth could I help if he became ill? This time I could not let him go so readily. I called for Blackwing who swooped down and in an instant we were flying together over the patchwork of gardens. Together we used our senses to track Blaize down, Blackwing with her shining black eyes and me with my sensitive nose tuned to the trail of bitter smoke. The evening air was full of other scents, fox and dog and cooking smells from the rows of houses, but on we flew until Blackwing suddenly swooped from the sky in a smooth and exhilarating arc.

I tumbled down from Blackwing's back and fell onto the ground, stopping Blaize in his tracks. He was out of breath. He was cross, spitting sparks coming from his hands and face. I held out my stone hand to him. He stepped back as though afraid, and I reached further. I put my hand into the fire of him. I felt heat, but no burn. The only pain that I could feel was his.

"Come back with us, Blaize, we will help you," I said to him.

He looked at me for a while, and then nodded, once. Bravely, Blackwing stood still as we both climbed atop her back. We settled, me in front, and Blaize with his smouldering, flaming arms around my stone waist.

"Home Blackwing," says I.

25th January

"It seems that you, me and the Fireboy have the same problem," said Dot. My frivolous friend talks so little of problems that my pointed ears pricked up immediately.

Blaize slept fitfully inside the earthen plantpot nearby, popping his head out in wakeful moments, his flaming features a picture of misery.

"And the problem is?" I asked casually. You have to be so careful with Dot. When she knows she has your full attention she is apt to drop it, to go off track or disappear altogether.

"We're alone. We've got nobody. All on our tods, that's us."

"Nonesense." says I, dismissively. "We have each other. We have Faith and George. We will never be rid of Blackwing!" I looked up to where Blackwing was sitting, perched like a guarding sentry atop the bars of Trampoline.

"But *really*, Bella. You know it's not right, hanging around humans, getting dressed up like a fancy toy! Whatever next, will you be building a little house, and planting a rose bush in the garden? We're not like them. And we're lost."

"You may well be lost, Dot," I told her, "but I most certainly am not."

"I'm going to show you something," she said to me, all the seriousness falling away from her demeanour in an instant. "Blackwing!" Blackwing swooped, and Dot climbed straight up onto her back. "Come on, then!" she said to me.

Feigning weariness, but secretly intrigued, I climbed up and found my comfortable place on Blackwing's back. Dot whispered something that I didn't quite catch, and then we were off. Her wing had healed perfectly and Blackwing's flight was now amazingly graceful. Straight up we went, towards the clouds. Was Dot taking me to see Crys? With no sign of snow I felt that this was unlikely, but I pinned the vague hope to my heart.

Sun streamed down through gaps in the clouds, partially blinding me, but Blackwing flew on. Up and up to where the air was clear and thin.

"Are you ready?" Dot shouted into my ear. I nodded, eagerly, and that was when she pushed me right off of Blackwing's back!

26th January

So, thanks to Dot and her outrageous behaviour, I find my wings to be not quite so useless after all. Such a shock was it that it seemed my friend was intent on murder, at first I did not feel the stirring, the crackling, and the spreading as my ancient folded wings were called to service. I fell and fell, gusts of wind carrying me sideways for a few moments, before I fell again. Down and down, dizzying circles towards the ground. I heard a laughing from above me, and Dot was falling, too. Her wobbly little legs were above me, kicking madly in the air. Her wings beat furiously, and she was struggling to catch her breath.

"You're flying Bella!" she shouted, and I was! I could find no words to say to her. She caught me up, and we were side by side in the air, with Blackwing a dark shadow overhead. We held hands and dodged the fat, cold raindrops that were falling with us.

"How did you know?" I asked Dot, eventually.

"I dint!" she answered as we fell fitfully, then gracefully earthwards.

She went off giggling soon after we landed. My wings work! So shocked I was for a while that I simply sat here, upon my pile of straw, looking occasionally to the House and sometimes to the plant pot where Blaize sleeps on. My wings work. I can fly!

When Faith came out with toasted sunflower seeds for us to share later on, I didn't tell her the news, but demonstrated instead. I climbed the wall quickly until I was level with her sparkling green eyes.

"Are you ready?" I asked of her. She nodded, and then off I went, fluttering upwards, across, around the garden and then back onto her outstretched hand.

"Oh, Arabella," she said, simply.

27th January

What to do with Blaize? He is grumpy and grizzly, and says few words.

The rain has turned to snow now, and he hunches inside the plant pot, cross with the delicate flakes that are occasionally blown in. They melt and hiss on contact with him.

"Are you hungry, Blaize?" I asked him today. "What do you eat?"

"Little girls made of stone!" he snapped back at me. This was a form of joke, I know. Maybe not the type of joke that I am used to, as neither one of us laughed, but I felt not the slightest bit worried that he might eat me. I sighed heavily, bewildered, not knowing what to do to make him happy.

"You should never have made that fire and woke me up," he grumbled.

"I'm sorry," I told him, and truly, I was.

28th January
Sleeping Blaize

Blaize has become slower and slower still, sleeping for hours at a time and not venturing out of the plant pot. Dot calls him a mornjy baby and has no time for his grumblings. Blackwing comes and watches over him from time to time, but it is hard to guess what the blackbird may be thinking. She is such a loyal bird. Those who have helped her have a friend for life! At a loss for how to help Blaize, though, I waited until dusk, when I knew that Faith would be home from school. My wings are becoming stronger everyday, and the short flutter to the top of the house followed by the cold, quick drop through the attic window is a far quicker journey than my previous scramble through the stone. I needed to chat with Faith, but she had not yet ventured up to her room. I braved the smell of rat urine, and played for a while with Alby in his cage. Looking up to the window from time to time as the day grew ever darker, I saw that a fluffy layer of snow now blocked out the dwindling light.

Faith finally arrived with Greta in tow, and I told her anxiously about Blaize and his worsening mood.

"I wouldn't have the faintest idea how to start to cheer such a little person up," Faith said to me, "but I would love to meet him."

Greta nodded her agreement.

The girls told Faith's mother that they had Science homework, and needed to collect leaves from the garden. As a result of this White Lie they were given permission to go out into the darkness.

I heard Faith's mother's voice from my hiding place deep within the anorak pocket.

"I hope this is not just a ruse to play in the snow! Don't

be out there too long, young lady. I don't want you missing school this week with a sore throat!"

Once out in the Garden, I led Greta and Faith to the upturned plant pot where Blaize had been skulking for the past few days. I should have known something was wrong, as Blackwing was perched on the wall above, shrilly squawking for all that she was worth.

I climbed the edge of the pot and looked inside, and the girls both crouched to investigate.

Inside the scorched pot there was nothing but a mounting fluff of snowflakes and the sad smell of smoking ash.

29th January
Cold Comfort

How I cried yesterday. You would not think that there could be so many tears worth of water stored inside a stone body. Faith did not want to leave me at all. When her mother called the girls in, she begged me to come back with her, but I could not bear to leave the smoky remains of my friend.

I sat there in the dark, becoming sadder and sadder as the faint trace of warmth that was Blaize cooled in the evening air. Blackwing came close to me, and I leaned against her frame, drawing comfort from the feathery contact. Soon the diminishing heat of Blaize was not even enough to melt the snowflakes, and they fell softly inside the plant pot covering every last trace of him.

"Blaize is dead, Blackwing," I told her. I searched her black eyes for a flicker of understanding, but could only see the murky grey reflection of myself.

"Arabella." I felt a cold hand on my shoulder, and whipped my head around in an instant. Crys! He was here in Faith's garden. Why I was so surprised is anyone's guess. Under any other circumstances, I would have been waiting and wishing and counting the snowflakes for his return.

The calm blue light that issued from his body illuminated a halo of soft flakes, floating dreamily around him in the darkness.

"My friend, Blaize, has died," I told Crys through my freezing tears.

"No, Arabella. I have been watching from the clouds. Blaize was tired, that is all. We Elementals cannot die. We change form. We sleep. Sometimes we sleep for an age, but we never die. Did your mother forget to tell you these truths?"

"I know so little, Crys." I confessed. "I do not even know where my Mother is."

"Then you must find her, little one. If she is Sleeping, then perhaps you should be Sleeping, too. I saw the green tips of spring flowers today, pushing through the frozen earth. Soon I too shall be sleeping through the warm season. I cannot bear to leave you like this, dear friend." I shivered at his icy touch as he wiped away my tears.

"Tell me where to find my Mother," I sobbed.

"I do not have all the answers, Arabella. You are more powerful than you think. Search your mind, and the answers may well be there."

"Please don't go," I begged of him.

"I have to go," he told me, "but I shall be back. We have until the end of time to get to know one another." With this he smiled gently, and each stage of the smile became a frozen picture in my mind. He kissed my cheek lightly. As I sit now, writing on my snowy pile of straw, I put my hand to that very same cheek. His kiss will always be there, I think, frozen in place, safe and timeless.

30th January
Plans

I have to find my Mother. There are other members of my family, as well. Why, oh why does my mind fail me so? Stone shapes rumble around on the outskirts of my unreliable memory. I looked to the moon last night, a glimmering sliver in the darkness. I asked no question of the faraway crescent, but felt a growing certainty within me that we were connected, the moon and I. The earth, too. The sky and the air. The fiery orb of the sun and the many friendly stars that have impartially looked on as I have made this amazing journey.

I need to return to the wall.

Today is Saturday which means no school for Faith and George. They were able to play out in the garden, enjoying the fun of the snow and the warmth of the sun all in one go! The snowfall was substantial enough for Faith to build a large snowman. He had oranges for eyes and an orange Felt Tipped Pen for a mouth. George was happy enough throwing handfuls of snow repeatedly into the air and watching the crystal particles fall down in the bright shards of sunlight.

As he watched the snow, his mother watched him from the open door of Dining Room. Concern crinkled her brow as George tirelessly played this repetitive game. Watching from the shadows of the wall, for the first time I felt pity for this short-tempered giantess. Eventually, George's favourite red gloves became completely sodden, and he screamed when his Mother tried to change them for a stripy blue pair. She calmed him, and led him back indoors, leaving me free to emerge from the depths of the wall.

I skipped into the air, light as a feather, and helped Faith complete the snowman, discarding the orange pen and moulding real features from the compacted snow. Faith gasped at my finished snowman model, and wondered aloud how she would explain this newfound talent to her parents.

It is late now, and the lights from the House have all been extinguished. Of course, I cannot sleep at all.

31st January
"Bella, they are everywhere!"

This is what Dot said to me when I asked her where she thought the rest of her people were.

"But I thought you said that you were alone. All on your tod, you said, I remember it clearly."

"Maybe I likes being alone." Dot said to me. She was making no sense at all.

"Well I know you won't like this, Dot, but I need to return to the stone wall where Faith and George first found me. I have to find my family."

"And whose idea is this?" Dot asked, bitterly. " That snowflake, Crys? Has he been floating around again? Fluffy little feather! Things are just fine as they are, Bella. We have lots of fun don't we, you, me, and Blackwing? With the big humanchilds lumbering around and taking us to Cinema, making us clothes and bringing us treats? There aint no wardrobe in an old dry stone wall for you to keep all your fancy gowns and capes in! What are you thinking of, going home? So much fun, we have here!"

"We do!" I agreed.

"So why change things? Maybe your Ma's gone off somewhere anyway. Maybe you got no Ma; you just dreamed her up."

"Dot! How could you say such a thing?" I tried to feel cross with her, but never had I seen my little friend so talkative and frantic. She really did not want me to go and I searched for the right words to comfort her.

"I could come back and visit."

She refused to comment and flapped her liquid wings, crossly.

"Come with me, then," I said, eventually.

She looked directly at me then, a tiny smile brightening her round face.

"There's a lake nearby this wall?" she asked tentatively.

"No….but I seem to recall a babbling brook!"

"I *may* come along for a little holiday," she said, the smile spreading a little.

"But how will we ever find the place?" I said to myself as I watched Blackwing hopping from branch to branch in the Sycamores.

"Well, I can count six working wings from where I'm standing," said Dot, with her hands on her hips.

Dot didn't really understand, though. A Car Journey can transport a person miles and miles in as many minutes. How long would it take our fragile, butterfly sized wings to retrace the journey from where Faith and George and first found me.

Dot and I played our splashing, flying and bouncing games until well into the night, and talked no more of holidays and babbling brooks. I will speak to Faith tomorrow, though. There must be a way to get back to The Wall.

1ˢᵗ February

Great news I have for you today, invisible reader! At once great and frightening. Faith and I were chatting in her bedroom earlier on today. I told her of my deep desire to return to the wall from whence I came. She was sad, my Faith was, but not cross. She seemed to understand. Family is so important to her, despite her mother's constant anxiety.

"Because of George, mainly," she told me, inclining her

conker-coloured head to the low-beamed eaves where George was playing a solitary game with a string of beads. I nodded my understanding and Faith said to me,

"If only I could persuade Mum and Dad that we need to revisit the cottage, the one near the wall where George found you. It's so hard to persuade Mum anything, she always thinks she knows best."

"Don't worry, Faith. I will find a way back to the wall one day," I said to her, with a smile.

"You liked that cottage, didn't you George? Do you remember when we were on holiday? You could go out to play in the garden. He went barefoot in the stream, even though it was October, and Dad built him his own rope swing on a big old Oak. Do you remember that holiday, George?"

A strange thing happened then. George, usually so distant and vague, stopped his bead-twizzling and stomped directly over to where Faith was sitting on her elegant bed. He came so close to her that she started to giggle. His eyes were pressed right up to hers.

"What are you doing, George?" Faith laughed, and all at once, George stopped this strange behaviour and went back to his twirling of the beads. Oh, so much to tell you have I, but the pen is heavy in my hand and the moon is hiding behind a mass of grey. Tomorrow! I will tell you then.

2nd February

So, to continue with my account of yesterday's excitement. Though George seemed interested in the holiday talks, Faith soon forgot all about this flicker of engagement, until she brought up the matter with her mother after tea.

"I loved that cottage, Mum, you know, the one in Northumbria?"

"Did you, Faith? I think George liked it there too."

"Yes, George loved it! I was so nice for him to be out doors and not having to hold someone's hand or be led by a wrist strap. Remember the rope-swing, George?" at this point in their conversation, George was picking at Chips and tasty Tomato Sauce, and seemed his usual oblivious self.

But, and this is the exciting part dear reader, his interest picked up again. He put down the sauce bottle and went to sit on his Mother's knee (something that he rarely does nowadays, according to Faith.) He looked deep into her eyes, and made sure that he had her attention, taking her face in his sturdy grip.

"HHHHoliday," he said in a voice that was as clear as a bell.

Neither Mother, Father nor Faith herself could believe that he had spoken! He is eight years old and never up until this point in time had he uttered so much as a word.

After a few tears of joy and surprise, Faith's mother insisted that her Father telephone the owners of the holiday cottage immediately, to see if there were any free weekends.

"If it is important enough to him to make him speak, Robert, then it is important enough for us to make plans around," she said firmly. Father was happy to comply, and did the telephoning duties. The cottage is free this very weekend and they are travelling in the Car on Friday, after school! Of course, I shall go, too, and Dot if she will, though I have not seen her today. Trying so hard to form a plan was I, and then the plan crept up on me and swept me away! I am nervous and fluttery, my wings with a crinkly life of their own. I cannot lie still. Mother, I am coming home.

3rd February

It is Wednesday today, I have tomorrow, and then the whole of Friday before our Car travel on Friday evening. I have not seen Dot at all since Sunday when she agreed to come home with me. Oh, where are you Dot? I cannot find her and I cannot sense her. Maybe she has changed her mind and gone back to her family, or her people, wherever they may be. Oh, how hard waiting is! I groom Blackwing every hour. I try to tell her that she must go back to being a wild bird once I am gone. She coos and responds so lovingly to my touch, adoration in her shiny black eyes. Whatever the reason for going, it is such a painful thing to leave your friends.

George has repeated the word 'holiday' four times since he first said it yesterday. He is determined for us all to return to that cottage! Faith's mother has dispensed with the dark cloak of mood that she is accustomed to wearing and has dug out some of her favourite music tapes. She dances around the house. She cooked a fancy dinner tonight (coconut chicken, said Faith, licking her lips) and she cannot wait for the weekend. I cannot wait neither.

4th February

The last one of my whole days here at Faith's Garden, and I am calm. All is arranged. I shall wear my travelling, adventuring clothes and the rest of my belongings shall be stored in Dolls' House, awaiting the return that surely I shall someday make.

There is little else to do but to look for Dot, who is mischievously hiding. I know she is somewhere nearby. I know many other things, too. I know that my mother is not afraid by my disappearance. She watches me somehow. She knows that I am safe, and she has enjoyed my adventure, but now she is calling me home. I cannot ignore the call of her voice, any more than Dot can ignore the call of a fluffy white cloud or a sparkling midnight lake.

Do you think me stiff and emotionless? I hope not, my friend, for that is certainly not the case. In Faith I have made a friend like no other, we are twin spirits, her and I, destined to meet again, many times. Of this we are both so sure that the certainty overrides our sadness. There is always a way. I will fly to her if I must, riding the many gusts of wind and stillness that form the oceans of space between us. I can travel through stone, through air, and through water. I will find her wherever she may be.

And Blackwing? What of my faithful bird-friend? Well, Blackwing needs to return to her wild state again, this much is clear to Faith and I both.

I fashioned sculptures from pebbles today, impressing the visions of my mind onto the soft, obedient stones. For Faith, a model of me on Blackwing's back, one wing shielding my eyes from the sun, the other fluttering raggedly behind.

And for Greta, a statuette of me and Dot together. Hard sculpting indeed to get stone to resemble a bubbling water person, but this I achieved. For Dot; nothing. There is nothing that she wants, only perhaps for me to be sorry for returning home. I can pretend, but in my heart I am not sorry. My journey had to come to an end someday.

Tonight, at last, I understand the messages that the stars are sending me with their light, sometimes bright and othertimes brighter. They tell me: "Live, Arabella Crumblestone. However you do it just live. And enjoy the living, too." I smile back at the friendly stars, and send them my own message.

"Thank you."

5th February
Home

I am pulled along by my mother's will and my heart's purpose. I rode quietly in Faith's pocket all throughout the car journey, feeling sad that Dot did not say her goodbyes or explain her change of mind.

Faith's mother and father chattered away about their holiday plans. They were happy. I knew that I had helped to make them happy. It was a strange thing, as they had never met me in person and did not know that I travelled alongside them. But in a way I had touched their lives.

George was his usual self. He played with a balloon throughout the journey, holding it by the end and bashing it onto the car seat in front. He bit it eventually, and it burst. His initial cry soon disappeared, when Mother said kindly, "Never mind, George. Holiday! We're going on Holiday!" George did not repeat the magical word, but hummed happily to himself, eyes closed and dreamy.

The car halted many times on our Journey.

"Blasted traffic!" Faith's father said, loudly.

"Robert, look at that," I heard Mother say, with interest. I listened and listened, not daring to peek out, but eager to find out what was so special and needed to be looked at.

"Blackwing!" Faith gasped, and then I just had to take a look, danger or none.

Blackwing it was! Perched like a proud, dark guardian on the front end of the car, looking straight in through the window. My friend refuses to leave me, even now! Well, I am glad. There is wilderness near the wall, and sufficient worms for her to feast on for the rest of her life, if she is determined to stay with me.

Faith herself stroked the top of my head with her fingers from time to time, to let me know that she was thinking of me. I knew anyway, but I leaned against the finger in fond embrace, to let her know the feelings in my heart.

When we arrived at the Cottage it was dark. I did not peek out of Faith's pocket to sniff the velvet night as the children and cases were ushered into the small, stone-built house. I felt my Mother's love all around. I was bathing in it, but I did not go to her at once. There was plenty of time, and for tonight I would stay with my friend. I snuggled up close to her in the unfamiliar bedroom. It took her many hours to fall to sleep, and we whispered our promises and secrets to one another well into the night. The window was open, allowing a fresh, crisp breeze to fill the room with loveliness. When at last Faith's eyelids settled and stilled, I climbed from the blankets, pulling them around her shoulders to protect her from the chill. I fluttered upwards to the open window and looked out to the wall. My wall! Tiny lights like stars fallen to earth floated dreamily in the darkness.

"Tomorrow", I whispered through the window.

6th February

Dear reader, I am home. But then, I have always been home, for the world is my home and the world is a small place when your wings are strong and your heart is open to adventure. This morning, with the Winter sun shrouded and peering like a misty faraway eye, Faith and I ventured into the chilly, dew-drenched day.

A Sheep, a large shaggy best, ambled up to us and peered closely at me. The caramel oblong eyes stirred a memory within me.

"Leroy?" I smiled up at the creature, and hitched a little ride within his clumpy matted fur. Straight to the very place that I needed to be, went he. Clever sheep!

"My Wall!" I exclaimed, and there it was in all its ancient craggy, moss-adorned glory. How can I explain to you? Is there a place that you have known so well that you forgot to consciously love it? Have you ever been away from that place for a while that seems like an eternity? Have you returned and felt the blood rush to your stone head and your newly working wings twitch with the beauty of it? If you never have then perhaps I cannot even attempt to explain.

"Mother!"

She emerged, a Stony Queen, from the wall. The morning sun twinkled in her old, old eyes. Her mossy hair was quite beautiful, laced as it was with fine silver strands. No scowl of disapproval marred her loveliness. She smiled with infinite understanding and acceptance.

"Arabella. My child," she said, and opened her stone arms. I ran to her. I embraced her. Father! Father was here with his chunky stone girth. And Grimble, and Dray, my little brothers. Forgiveness it was not, for my family understood completely that I had been compelled to go forth unto the world.

"I forgot so much, Mother" It told her as I hugged her.

"You were always forgetful!" she said. "But your Sleep was disturbed. That is never a good thing, Arabella. If you must go Adventuring, be sure to sleep first. My sweet girl." She kissed the top of my head over and over. I thought to show her my working wings, but she just nodded, patiently. She already knew! She knew everything, and she questioned nothing.

"I been wondering when you'd arrive," said a familiar voice.

"Dot!"

"Yes, Dot! That's my name! Lovely little brook over here, come in for a swim, why don't you? I might stay on for a holiday extension!" Dot said, gleefully. Mother rolled her eyes (it seemed that the pair of them were already well acquainted).

"Have you any more interesting friends for me to meet?" Mother asked, playfully, as the dark shadow of Blackwing fell upon us.

"Dot is a dear friend. And Blackwing too. You must meet Faith, and her brother, George. Oh, I have so much to tell you," I rambled.

"And the snow is coming…" Mother said.

"Yes" says I, "the snow."

7th February

"Do you know the faeries of the snow?" I asked my Mother.

"I know all of the faeries, my darling. Why do you ask about the Snow Folk, in particular?"

"I met someone." Mother raised a velvet green eyebrow in question.

"You will meet many people, Arabella," she told me. "Look". Mother gestured towards the dying day, where misty sunlight still hovered in places.

"Look at what?"

"Oh, daughter. Look harder. *See!*"

At her words my eyes opened fully. Faeries were everywhere! Tree faeries, willowy and graceful. Faeries of the earth, the ground, the roots. Faeries of the very air, nothing to them but wisps and smiles and gentleness. Each plant has a faerie, each creature and each twinkling star. I looked at Dot, who was swimming in the babbling brook.

"Ah" I said. "They are everywhere."

Dear Arabella,

My beautiful friend. Thank you so much for the gift of your diary. I will treasure it always. My family and I will be returning to the cottage in the Autumn, and in the Spring. It is a very special place to us all. To me, of course, because it is where I met you. To George, for who-knows-what-reason, and to Mum and Dad, because here they finally learned to be happy. We will see each other often, I think, Arabella, though I know you are not made to live in my world. Though your wings are delicate, I know that you are strong, and if you need me you will find a way. You have Blackwing, who will always be grateful for the way that you nursed her back to health. You have Dot, who (although very probably crazy) is also your loyal friend. You have me, Arabella. You will always have me.
I will treasure the diary, and your rail of clothes is waiting for you in Dolls' House. I have new designs!

Take care, my precious one,

Faith Raymondson
Xxx

The End

About the Author

Sharon King is first and most importantly a Mum. Her youngest two children, Daisy and Lenny, have severe disabilities, and because of this fact, she expects to be a Mum until the day that she dies. Although this prospect fills her with peace and happiness instead of dread, to be able to fit in a little writing along the way is a luxury that she intends to make the most of.

About the Illustrator

Rose King is twelve years old and lives in Wakefield, West Yorkshire with her parents and two younger siblings.

These are her first professional illustrations.

Like George in the story, Rose has a form of autism. She is confident and strong, and has always been proud of her Asperger's Syndrome. She feels that it is an essential part of who she is. Her definition of autism is "a type of awesomeness".

Rose very much hopes that you enjoy the story.